The full moon still calls your name

Nour Lorenzo

Author: Nour Lorenzo

Cover design: Nour Lorenzo

ISBN paperback: 978-1-7375545-6-1

ISBN ebook: 978-1-7375545-5-4

For you, who were and will be my beacon of
light in the darkest nights,

despite everything — distance and years.

Inspired by a true story.

1

The plane landed after a five-hour flight. It was seven in the evening, and through the window, the sun was slowly setting. A golden light bathed the runway, and the palm leaves swayed in the wind. As I looked around, a sense of fear and uncertainty washed over me. I would be spending the next month doing my medical internship at one of Amman's hospitals, but what my days would be like there was still a mystery. A knot formed in my stomach. I took a deep breath. It was too late to turn back.

Little by little, the plane emptied, and I had no choice but to step out. I walked down the ramp into the terminal, which looked quite similar to many others I had been through. I looked for the baggage claim sign and, following the rest of the passengers, walked down long carpeted corridors dimly lit, surrounded by the murmur of foreign conversations and the rolling sound of carry-on suitcases. Like in any international terminal, before picking up the luggage, we had to go through customs and visa control.

While waiting for my turn, I was struck by the clothing and appearance of the people around me, very different from what I was used to. Many of the women covered their heads with a scarf and wore dark-toned robes that concealed everything except their eyes, reducing them to a silhouette. Most of them hid behind sunglasses, and those who didn't had perfectly done makeup, their eyes sharply outlined in black. As for the men, there were fewer of them, and they also wore robes. Theirs reached down to the ankles and, unlike the women's, were almost always a pristine white. Some complemented theirs with a red-and-white checkered scarf held in place by a black cord. I would later learn the names of these garments. The scarf covering the women's heads is called a hijab, and the robes are known as niqab. If the garment covered the entire face, it was called a burqa. As for the men, the red scarf is called a *keffiyeh* or *shemagh*, and along with the white robe, it's a traditional outfit commonly seen in Saudi Arabia.

Then there were us Western travelers. There were the typical backpackers, with their rugged look, hauling massive backpacks and hiking boots tied to the outside. I pictured their passports filled with stamps and wondered where they were coming from or heading to. Maybe they were returning from Burma or Indonesia or some other exotic place. Or maybe they had just left home, although, judging by their appearance, it looked like they had been wandering the world for weeks. There were couples, probably on their honeymoon, behaving affectionately, seemingly in search of a "One Thousand and One Nights" kind of love story. And then, there was the last group: those traveling alone, buried in their phone screens like me. I wondered what they thought of me.

After waiting for a little over fifteen minutes in line, it was finally my turn with the visa officer. No complications, barely any questions, and twenty Jordanian dinars later, he stamped one of the many blank pages in my passport. Apparently, that stamp was my visa.

"Welcome to Jordan!" he said with a brief smile. "Next!" With a quick motion, he called the person behind me, not giving me a chance to respond.

"One more step toward the adventure," I thought, and I went down the escalator toward baggage claim. I let out a breath of relief when I saw my suitcase appear on the conveyor belt, easily recognizable by the red ribbon tied to it. My dad had given me that tip years ago so I wouldn't mistake it for someone else's. It had helped me more than once. I looked for the exit door and slowly made my way toward it, trying to delay the moment. On the other side, Mohammed would be waiting. I was eager to meet him in person, but I couldn't help feeling nervous.

Mohammed was the medical student assigned as my guide for the month, and we had been communicating through emails and Facebook during that time. He had helped me with the paperwork and had also given me some "foreigner tips," as he called them, mostly related to dress code and etiquette. Aside from guiding me on those things, he was supposed to meet me at the airport and assist me with anything I might need during the first few days.

As I walked toward the exit, I reminded myself of one of those etiquette rules: I should greet him with a handshake only, no kisses. I was used to Spain, where we give a kiss on each cheek, and with how tired I was, muscle memory could easily lead me into an awkward situation. I took a deep breath and walked through the "Arrivals" door, where metal railings formed a narrow corridor. I have to admit, that moment made me uncomfortable. Even for just a few seconds, I felt everyone's eyes on me, and I didn't like being the center of attention.

Among all the people waiting, I looked for Mohammed, who had told me he would be holding a sign with my name. Fortunately, it wasn't hard to spot him. In fact, I wouldn't have needed a sign at all. Mohammed had a distinctive look, and with the photos I had seen on his Facebook profile, I would've recognized him anyway. He was tall, almost 6 feet 5 inches, and carried a bit of extra weight. He had a kind expression, a round face, and a thick beard. He was wearing a red tracksuit and stood out from the crowd. He looked tired, but his face lit up when he saw me. I wondered how long he had been waiting.

With a smile and a handshake, he welcomed me. He quickly grabbed my suitcase. I thanked him and followed his long strides toward the parking lot, which was just outside the terminal, in the open air.

The breeze was warm, and night had already fallen. The parking lot was lined with palm trees. We walked between the parked cars until we reached a black Toyota Camry. He opened the passenger door, inviting me in. After placing my suitcase in the trunk, he got into the car, which trembled slightly for a few seconds. Mohammed was huge, and he had to tilt the driver's seat back to be able to sit and drive somewhat comfortably. That car was definitely one size too small for him. He turned on the radio and started singing. It seemed to be one of that summer's hit songs, and it had a catchy rhythm. He smiled and started driving. We pulled out of the parking lot, and little by little, I began to relax. Mohammed seemed like a good guy.

After about half an hour on the highway, we could see the outskirts of Amman on the horizon, and before long, we were driving into the city. The avenue we were on had no lane markings, and the cars seemed to guide each other by honking. There were barely any traffic lights and even fewer crosswalks. He explained that traffic was like that in most streets and that pedestrians had to be bold and just step out, hoping the cars would stop. It seemed dangerous to me, and I was surprised by how little road safety there was in the city. There were no sidewalks either, and in many sections, people had to walk along the shoulder. On the other hand, the streets were quite well lit, and most houses had a beige-brown color, as if painted with desert sand. I also noticed the shop signs, written in Arabic script, completely unreadable to me. One billboard in particular caught my attention, a Coca-Cola ad I wouldn't have recognized if it weren't for the brand's iconic logo. Their alphabet was truly different from ours.

During the ride, Mohammed told me interesting facts and answered my questions before I could even ask them. It was like he could read my mind and knew exactly what would catch my attention. Maybe I wasn't the first student he had hosted, and my curiosity was easy to predict. Staying true to his warm hospitality, he insisted on treating me to dinner somewhere special. He took me to the heart of Amman, or Downtown, one of the city's most iconic and touristy areas. It was lively, and the main street was crowded. To my surprise, nearly everyone there was a man. The few women present were accompanied by their husbands and wore dark robes that covered them almost completely.

"This is the old part of the city, and although it's pretty touristy, it's still one of the most conservative areas," said Mohammed, once again reading my mind.

He parked a couple of blocks before the main street. We walked for a few minutes toward the noise and bustle. It felt like all the life of the city was concentrated there. Even though it was already nine at night, the market was still open and buzzing with activity. Tourists and locals blended into a diverse mix. The locals seemed used to foreigners, though curious glances were occasionally cast, mostly at Western women dressed in more revealing clothing. The street was filled with small souvenir shops, most of them tiny, with vendors standing at the entrances inviting passersby to come inside. There were also many restaurants, their outdoor terraces packed with locals and tourists enjoying dinner. The sounds of people and the smell of spices filled the air.

Mohammed chose one of the city's most famous restaurants, a humble-looking spot that nonetheless held a great reputation. It proudly displayed photos of famous customers on the walls, including the King of Jordan. He was smiling next to what may have been the restaurant owner. We sat on the terrace.

The white plastic chairs and tables reminded me of the beach bars in southern Spain.

The restaurant specialized in *falafel*, one of Jordan's most popular dishes, something like a chickpea fritter with spices. It was served in a round, flat bread typical of the region called *pita bread*. I had never tried that kind of food before, and to my surprise, it was delicious. I didn't leave a single crumb, and Mohammed smiled with satisfaction at how quickly I devoured it.

While I waited for him to finish his third *falafel* sandwich, I looked around and noticed how different Amman was from my own city. I felt out of place, yet somehow welcomed at the same time. I sensed an unexpected familiarity, as if I had more in common with that place than I'd thought, despite the distance and cultural differences. I was excited to explore the country and make the most of this experience that fate had given me.

After dinner, we took a quick walk through the market, but we didn't stay long; it was getting late. Besides, it had been a long trip, and I was exhausted. We got back in the car and headed toward the apartment. On the way, I kept looking at the streets, the buildings, the people... Everything stirred my curiosity. We left the noise behind and arrived at what would be my neighborhood, much quieter and more modern than Downtown.

Mohammed turned right onto a residential street lined with trees and cars parked on both sides. It was deserted. He drove down it slowly and stopped near the end, we had arrived. He parked and helped me with my luggage. He pointed to the building as he walked toward it, and I followed a few steps behind. The front door was slightly ajar, so Mohammed pushed it open with ease. The entryway was dark and narrow. He switched on the light, which barely illuminated a corridor of gray tiles that gave off a somewhat eerie vibe. I was glad he was there with me.

We walked down the corridor in silence until we reached the second-to-last door on the left. He opened it and turned on the light, motioning for me to enter. I was surprised by how small the studio was and by the fact that, despite its size, it had three beds. That's when I realized it wasn't just for me. I'd be sharing it with two other people. I knew other foreign girls were coming, but I hadn't expected we'd all be living in the same place. I wondered how we would manage in those thirty square meters. It felt more like a single room than an apartment, serving every purpose and none at the same time.

I put my things in a corner and chose the bed in the far end, the one that offered the most privacy. He handed me the apartment keys and explained the building's schedule. Apparently, the main entrance closed at ten at night and opened at eight in the morning; outside those hours, I'd have to use the garage to come and go. He also filled me in on other neighborhood details, from where to find Wi-Fi to where to shop and how to catch a taxi in the mornings for the hospital. His eyes were practically closing from exhaustion, and mine were too.

"Do you have any questions?" he asked, stifling a yawn. "Well, if you need anything, just call me. You have my number!" he went on as he headed for the door. "*Layla Saida!*" he said, wishing me good night in Arabic.

14

"Thank you so much for everything. I don't think I have any questions," I replied, trying not to yawn as well.

"I'll come pick you up at seven tomorrow evening. A few of us from the group are getting together for a drink. Everyone's looking forward to meeting you!" he smiled before closing the door.

I listened to his footsteps fade away down the hallway, and then the night went silent. I slid the bolt on the door. I went to the bathroom and looked into the small mirror above the sink. I had dark circles under my eyes and looked exhausted; I really needed some sleep.

I opened my suitcase, looking for my pajamas. My clothes were cold and had that hint of dampness they always seemed to pick up when traveling from one place to another. It felt like I was bringing a piece of Asturias with me. I took off my clothes, dropped them on the floor, and took a hot shower, as quick as the trickle of water would allow. Then I got into bed and curled up under the blanket. I closed my eyes and pictured my mother hugging me. I missed her. Before switching off the light, I noticed the window had its blinds lowered. It was the first time I'd seen the same characteristic Spanish blinds outside of Spain. Exhaustion pulled me into a deep sleep before I had the chance to miss my own bed.

2

The red hues of the sunset blended with the sunbaked facades of the buildings. From the window, the empty street could be seen, and the soft breeze gently stroked the tree branches. Calm reigned. In the distance, the echo of the muezzin calling to prayer could be heard, one of the signature sounds of the city.

Mohammed was about to arrive, and as usual, I was getting ready in a rush. I wasn't quite sure what to wear. I still didn't fully understand what was considered socially acceptable clothing and was afraid of dressing inappropriately and making a bad first impression. In the end, after discarding several outfits, I settled on a long black dress that reached the floor and a denim jacket that covered my arms. That combo couldn't go wrong. Just as I was finishing my makeup, I got a message from Mohammed saying he had arrived. It was exactly seven o'clock. I put on my sandals and hurried out of the house. He was double parked and smiled when he saw me. He got out of the car to greet me and open the door. This time, he was more dressed up, dark jeans and a blue polo shirt that emphasized his belly. His hair was neatly slicked back, and his beard had been freshly trimmed.

Along the way, just like the day before, he answered all my questions and told me more about the city and the hospital where I would be doing my internship. What surprised me most was the difference in the workweek: Sundays were their Mondays, and the weekend started Thursday afternoon.

Besides talking about Amman and the Jordanian world, we also had time to talk about Spain. Mohammed loved soccer and was a huge fan of the Spanish league, especially Real Madrid. I discovered he knew better than I did which teams were in the first division and what their lineups were. He even remembered which teams had been relegated to second division the previous season. He knew about my hometown team, Real Sporting de Gijón, just because they had tied with Real Madrid a couple of years ago. I was struck by the reach of Spanish soccer in such a faraway place.

We arrived in Abdoun, one of the most modern neighborhoods in Amman, completely different from Downtown. This area housed embassies and consulates, as well as the city's most important hotels. There were also restaurants and bars that served alcohol. According to Mohammed, it was like a small version of the West within the city.

That night, we had plans to meet at Seven Bottles, one of the trendiest places in town. A line of people was waiting outside.

It looked like it was at full capacity. Luckily, the line wasn't long, barely ten people ahead of us. I studied them as the line moved forward. Most were probably in their twenties or thirties, and based on their appearance, they could've easily blended into a night out in Gijón or Madrid. In fact, some of the girls were wearing outfits my mother would've definitely found too provocative. It was fascinating to observe the contrasts in that city.

It didn't take long to get in, and I quickly understood why this was such a popular bar. Inside, there was a courtyard with tables surrounding a white stone fountain. The white walls were covered in hanging plants, and giant potted palm trees decorated the corners. It was a beautiful place. Rihanna was playing, and the whole atmosphere radiated joy. Everyone was enjoying the start of the weekend. Among the crowd, at a table in the back, was our group of students, about ten of them. It looked like we were among the last to arrive.

"There they are! Almost everyone's here!" Mohammed said, raising his arms as he walked toward them.

A knot formed in my stomach. I always found it hard to be myself and come up with conversation topics when I didn't know anyone in a group. Doing it in another language made it even more difficult. One by one, Mohammed introduced me to everyone, and they all greeted me with smiles. Most of their names were new to me, and between the nerves and the music, I forgot them as soon as they were said.

The group was made up of several foreign exchange students like me and some locals, Mohammed's classmates from medical school. All the Jordanians were part of the exchange program and would act as guides and coordinators to ensure our experience over the next four weeks would be smooth and enjoyable.

We sat at one of the open corners of the table. I wasn't sure what everyone else was drinking, and when the waiter came, afraid of standing out, I ordered a lemonade instead of a cocktail. The conversation flowed easily among them, and they all seemed to have a million things in common or to talk about. Meanwhile, I struggled to keep up with their chats and jokes. Often, when they laughed, even if I didn't quite understand why, I laughed too. I did it out of embarrassment, trying to hide my lack of comprehension. Other times, it was obvious I didn't know what they were talking about, and they patiently repeated and explained things until I understood. Luckily, there was a Chilean girl, Sofía, who quickly became my official translator for the night. We hit it off instantly, and she wasted no time telling me her story. She had been born in Santiago, and when she was just five, her family emigrated to San Diego. She had lived her whole life in California until she moved to Chicago to study medicine. Sofía was short and dark-haired, with a sincere smile and green eyes. She had inherited her Arab features from her grandfather, a Palestinian refugee who had fled to South America in the 1950s.

After a while, another local student arrived. He was tall and athletic, with short, curly black hair, a perfectly groomed beard, and thick eyebrows framing his gaze. His sun-kissed skin contrasted sharply with his crisp white shirt, whose top two buttons were undone to reveal his neck and a hint of chest. He reminded me of guys from the south, and I felt an instant attraction.

He greeted everyone with hugs or handshakes, starting at the end of the table nearest the entrance, on the opposite side from where I was sitting. He seemed quite popular; everyone lit up when they saw him. I watched from the corner of my eye, hoping someone would introduce us. Our eyes met briefly, just long enough to confirm that he'd noticed me too.

Sofía, who'd arrived a week earlier, already knew him, and they hugged. Sitting beside me, she introduced us. This time, I had no trouble remembering his name: Yazid. Close up, his eyes were even more captivating, and I felt my nerves tingle. His presence was striking, like someone straight out of a cologne ad.

"Welcome to Jordan," he said with a smile, looking right at me. "How is your trip so far?"

His voice was deep and velvety, every bit as magnetic as his appearance. I prayed my body language didn't betray my flustered state. I forced myself to focus on speaking English and on the conversation, even as I felt drawn to him. He told me he'd just completed medical school and was one of the oldest in the group.

Yazid was warm and insisted on buying me a drink. I wasn't sure if it was pure hospitality or something more, since none of the other Jordanians had offered. Still, I accepted. Without waiting for the waiter, he looped his arm through mine and led me toward the bar.

The music was loud, and the bar was packed, most people dancing in clusters. We navigated through the crowd until we reached the counter. Leaning close, he asked what I wanted, and his cologne enveloped me. A unique scent that made me even more drawn to him. I gave a vague nod, too distracted to speak. He smiled and placed our order while I stood there, soaking in the atmosphere. You'd never guess we were in a Middle Eastern city.

A few minutes later, he handed me a blue cocktail called Azraq, which means "blue" in Arabic. We made our way back to the terrace, Yazid clearing a path and casually holding my hand, letting go just before we stepped outside so no one would notice. Back at the table, the Jordanian girls shot us curious glances, perhaps a bit of envy. Sofía looked over but said nothing. Unsure how to read their reactions, I chose to ignore them.

The rest of the night passed peacefully. Yazid and I exchanged a few more glances, but spoke only within the group. I felt myself loosening up in English, though I was still far from expressing myself fully. I wondered what first impression I'd made.

It was barely eleven when we began saying our goodbyes, nightlife here ends much earlier than in Spain. Yazid came over and hugged me.

"Nice to meet you, Lola," he whispered. "See you soon." And with that, he slipped away.

His scent lingered with me until morning. Mohammed drove Sofía and me home, her apartment was next door to mine. She'd gotten lucky; her place had only one bed. I couldn't imagine how small it was, but at least it was hers alone. Honestly, I was a bit excited to meet my future roommates. According to

Mohammed, one was from Sweden and the other from Norway. I'd never met anyone from Northern Europe. It sounded intriguing.

I changed into my pajamas and climbed into the narrow bed against the wall. In the dim light, just before sleep, my thoughts drifted to Daniel, and I felt a thrilling fear of myself.

3

It was Thursday afternoon, and the weekend was beginning. After finishing at the hospital, and before meeting up with the rest of the group, Harita, Sofía, and I went to Rainbow Street. Lined with restaurants and shops, it was one of the most popular streets in Amman, especially among tourists. We were starving, and following Mohammed's recommendation, we grabbed a falafel sandwich at Al-Quds. It was a tiny, traditional place. Through the window, we could see them frying the falafel in a massive vat of boiling oil. We wandered slowly down the street, eating our sandwiches and looking at the shop windows. It was still early, so to kill time before our meetup with the Jordanians, we stopped at *Sufra Café* for iced tea. It had a rooftop terrace, and we chose to sit in some armchairs facing Downtown. The view was beautiful.

From the first day we met, the three of us had done everything together. Elsa, the fourth member of our group, wasn't with us today. She usually joined our plans, but that afternoon she had made plans with her newly found Jordanian love. We were all very different from one another, but we complemented each other surprisingly well and made a great quartet. We loved exploring the city together. I felt lucky to be sharing this experience with them.

Harita was Norwegian, but of Indian heritage, her parents had emigrated from northern India, near Kashmir, just forty years ago. Although she had grown up in a progressive country, she was still bound by the cultural traditions of her parents and by Sikhism, a minority religion known for its strict and traditional values, which her parents followed to the letter. They wanted Harita to marry someone from the same religion, which significantly limited her options, since there were barely any Sikhs in Norway. One aspect of her faith that stood out to me was their reverence for hair, considered a gift from God and, as such, not to be cut. Men wore their hair hidden under turbans. Beyond this exotic and unfamiliar religion, what impressed me most about Harita was her intelligence. She was in her early twenties, like me, but had already traveled across five continents and needed both hands to count the languages she spoke. She had olive-toned skin, and her straight hair reached nearly all the way down her back. One of her quirks was sleeping with the air conditioning on full blast. Maybe she missed the cold of Norway, or maybe she just liked curling up under the blankets. But it made my nose freeze, and every night we negotiated the temperature. I hated the dry, cold air from that unit.

Then there was Elsa, one hundred percent Swedish. Tall and sturdy, with pale skin and fine blond hair. She hid behind large square-framed glasses and laughed loudly, never caring if people stared. Elsa was close to thirty, though sometimes her wild behavior reminded me of a fifteen-year-old. She liked to wander off on her own in the mornings to find Wi-Fi before heading to the hospital. Somehow, by her second day in Amman, she had already met a Jordanian guy named Syed. She had fallen in love at first sight and had begun skipping out on our plans, like that afternoon. She said he treated her in a way no man ever had, that with him she felt protected. She compared him to Swedish guys and claimed they had lost their sense of romance, that they were all too cold and not masculine enough, not like the Jordanian. Maybe she was right.

And then there was Sofía, the American student of Chilean origin who had grown up in California. By far, she was the most outgoing of the group, and within just a few days she had made friends with all the students participating in the exchange. She came from a traditional Christian family, but her horizons were broader. Instead of following in her mother's footsteps and marrying young, she had decided to become a doctor. She wanted to specialize in International Cooperation and travel with NGOs to third-world countries to help the most vulnerable. Sofía was also deeply curious about Arab culture, perhaps inspired by her grandfather, who had been a Palestinian refugee who fled to South America in the 1950s. She was learning Arabic and practiced it every chance she got. The Jordanians really appreciated her efforts, which made them like her even more. Sometimes I felt a healthy kind of envy: she spoke perfect English, had a natural gift with people, and could strike up a conversation with anyone, unlike me.

There we were, sipping iced tea and smoking hookah on Sufra's terrace. We'd chosen watermelon flavor and passed it around as we chatted. I loved that fleeting dizziness I felt after a few deep puffs. Words became heavy on my tongue, and I would just smile and sink into the couch while listening to the others.

"Girls, we have to head to Zafra Café soon," Sofía said, checking her watch. "We're meeting the Jordanians at eight."

"Let's ask for the check," said Harita. "Do you know if Elsa's coming?"

"No idea. I think she's with Syed," I replied. "I don't think she'll show up tonight."

"She's lost her mind," Harita said with a worried frown. "I hope she's okay."

"She's a grown woman. Don't worry," I said, trying to reassure her.

Elsa had disappeared with her Jordanian, and we all knew she wouldn't be back until that night. She was truly in love and let herself go with her emotions without resistance. I thought it was an act of courage.

We finished our tea, and I took a few last puffs from the hookah. Then we got in a taxi heading to Downtown, where Zafra Café was. Another of the city's most famous and iconic restaurants. That place appeared in every travel guide and was crowded with both locals and tourists, who came to enjoy live music and traditional Arab dishes.

The Jordanians were more punctual than I'd expected, they were already there. Or perhaps we were simply late. Among them, to my surprise, was Yazid. A shiver ran down my spine. I hadn't seen him since our first encounter. I knew we'd run into each other eventually, but I hadn't imagined it would be that night. He was wearing a light blue shirt, similar in style to the one before, with the top two buttons undone and the sleeves rolled up. He had on the same brown loafers I remembered from the first night, the ones that gleamed so sharply. I couldn't deny he had style.

Yazid smiled when he saw me. We greeted each other with a hug, and once again, his cologne lingered in the air. I did my best to hide how nervous I felt. He seemed indifferent, barely changing his expression when he looked at me. Just before we stepped into the café, he gently took hold of my arm to get my attention.

"Hey, Lola. I need to buy some tobacco. The shop's about a five-minute walk from here," he said with a grin. "Want to come along?"

"Yeah, sure," I replied, caught off guard once again.

The others looked a bit surprised too, probably reminded of that first night. I wasn't sure what to think, but I couldn't deny the pull I felt toward him. We slipped away into the crowd, and once we were out of sight, he took my hand again. He had a habit of doing that, as if it were the most natural thing in the world.

Maybe it was becoming natural for me too. For some reason, I didn't resist. My steps felt light, as if I were floating.

We talked about nothing in particular; my first few days at the hospital, his plans to spend the summer in Amman, how relieved he felt after finally finishing six long years of medical school.

Every now and then, he'd pause to say something or ask a question, fixing his intense black eyes on me. It was hard to focus on what he was saying. I had to really concentrate not to lose track of the conversation.

We walked slowly, savoring the stroll and the rare moment alone. We took longer than expected to return, and honestly, I could've talked with him all night. I wouldn't have minded skipping Zafra altogether and going somewhere else, just the two of us. There was something magnetic about his presence.

As soon as we got back to the group, Yazid returned to his usual reserve. He spoke to me when it made sense in the conversation but kept his distance. I still couldn't figure out how to read him. On the ride home, Harita and Sofía teased me about Yazid, but since they knew about Daniel, they didn't press the subject or make a big deal out of it.

That night, I went to bed thinking of Daniel again. I felt guilty for being so easily impressed, for starting to feel something for a man who had been a stranger just a week earlier. What made it worse was that I didn't miss Daniel as much as I'd expected. He was off on a maritime expedition across the Atlantic aboard a training ship called *Creoula*. He barely had reception, and certainly no Wi-Fi. Our communication had shrunk to brief, off-timed messages. That made it easier for my attention to drift toward Yazid.

At the same time, I was still upset with Daniel for choosing that trip over coming to Jordan with me. It felt like yet another sign of how disconnected he was, how little interest he showed in our relationship. I knew I was being selfish, and that I needed to respect his freedom and his choices. But still, it was hard to accept. I took refuge in those thoughts as a way to excuse what I was beginning to feel for Yazid.

4

As soon as the sun rose, we set off. The Jordanians had planned a weekend trip to the south of the country, and there was no time to waste. First, we would visit the ruins of Petra, then spend the night in the Wadi Rum desert, and the following day, explore the Red Sea. I couldn't wait to see it all, especially Petra, the eighth wonder of the ancient world. I had read about it and seen countless photos of its rock-carved facades. On many cold, rainy study days, I had escaped by imagining myself there. That moment had finally come.

The Jordanians had split us up among several cars, and luckily, Sofía, Harita, Elsa, and I ended up in Yazid's. The others, two Americans, a Dutch guy, and a German student who had arrived just a few days earlier, rode in the other vehicles. The three-hour drive gave us plenty of time to talk about all sorts of things, but Petra remained the central topic. We had all read up on it and kept cross-checking facts while peppering Yazid with questions. Despite being focused on driving, he answered them all without hesitation, no matter how obscure or detailed they were.

According to Yazid, Petra was also known as the Rose City or the Lost City, and its history was truly fascinating. Though it now felt remote, it had once been a vital commercial center thanks to its strategic position on the trade routes to Asia. It also had a water distribution system that supplied merchants after their long journeys, making it even more appealing. But everything changed when the Romans defeated the Nabataeans and annexed Petra into the Roman Empire in 106 AD. Around that time, maritime routes to Asia began to flourish, gradually overshadowing the overland trade routes—and Petra with them. To make matters worse, a major earthquake in the 4th century AD caused severe damage, and the city was eventually abandoned.

After many years lost to time, Petra was rediscovered by Johann Ludwig Burckhardt, a Swiss man who had fallen in love with Arab culture and converted to Islam. But before Johann arrived, Bedouins, another nomadic desert tribe like the Nabataeans, had already settled there. Following its rediscovery, Petra slowly gained recognition. It was eventually named a UNESCO World Heritage Site, and the Bedouins had to leave and relocate to the surrounding areas. Still, they adapted well. Though they no longer lived in Petra, many made tourism their way of life by opening restaurants or souvenir shops nearby.

34

As Yazid told the story, the sunlight poured in through the window, casting light on his profile. His jaw was prominent, yet perfectly balanced with his nose. The more I studied his features, the more attractive he seemed. He gave off an air of quiet confidence, perhaps that's what I found most appealing. I wondered what he thought of me. His behavior over the past few days had left me confused. I still didn't understand why he had invited me for a drink or asked me to walk with him to buy tobacco. Now he was acting indifferent again, which only added to my uncertainty.

While I was lost in these thoughts, Harita, satisfied with the Petra lecture, changed the subject.

"By the way, Yazid, you just graduated, right? How does it work here?" she asked. "Do you do an internship first, or go straight into residency?"

"I start my internship in September. It lasts one year," he said. After a brief pause, he added, "Then I plan to move to the U.S. and apply for a residency in orthopedics. I have family there, and it's a great place to train." He said it calmly, almost like a practiced response.

"That's awesome!" said Sofía. "You should totally come to Chicago. It's a great city with tons of hospitals. Plus, there's a big Arab community. You'd feel right at home."

"Yeah, Chicago would be great, honestly. But you know how it goes: first you send your resume, then come the interviews… It's tough, but yeah, Chicago is definitely a solid option."

"That sounds like such a long process!" I said, surprised. "In Spain, everything depends on a single exam: no resumes, no interviews. The student chooses, and the hospital has no say in who gets in or not."

"Americans love to complicate things," Yazid joked. This time, he glanced away from the road just long enough to flash me a smile.

The flat desert gave way to rising mountains. Nestled among them was the Arabah Valley, home to Petra. We passed a sign marking the final turnoff to the visitor parking lot. There were barely any spots left, cars and buses filled the area. We had arrived. I was bursting with excitement to finally see that legendary place.

It was scorching hot, and the sun made walking feel like a challenge. We applied sunscreen and grabbed our backpacks. The Jordanians wrapped *keffiyehs*, the traditional red-and-white checkered scarves, around their heads. Besides shielding them from the sun, the scarves also symbolized solidarity with the Palestinian people. Wearing one was a form of protest against the Israeli occupation. Nearly all of them had Palestinian roots; their families had come to Jordan years ago, fleeing the conflict.

After buying our tickets at the entrance, we stopped by a fast-food stall just before the gate to grab something similar to a *kebab*. We ate while walking, barely stopping, since it was already getting late and there was so much to see.

We began our visit at the Siq, the narrow stone gorge that leads into the plaza where the ancient city of Petra truly begins. There, carved into the sandstone, stood the magnificent

Treasury. After crossing the plaza, we ventured deeper into the city, letting ourselves be swept away by its beauty. There was so much to see—from the famous tombs and the grand Nabataean temple to the colonnaded street, a legacy left behind by the Romans. We kept walking, and after climbing hundreds of steps, we reached the Monastery. Like the Treasury, it was carved into the rock, but even larger and more spectacular. It was, without a doubt, a magical place.

Exhausted from the heat and the distance we had covered, we sat on a stone ledge to take in the view. There were hardly any tourists around, and the silence was broken only by the wind. Enchanted by the beauty of that place, we lost all sense of time. As darkness began to fall, we knew it was time to head back.

Night fell as we descended the steps, and just when we thought we'd have to walk back in the dark, we came across a group of Bedouins. They were used to late tourists like us and, for a few dinars, offered to take us to the parking lot in their pickup. It was an improvised ride, the bed of the truck was nothing more than an open cargo area without seats. Covered in dust and sweat, we piled in, laughing and chatting about how breathtaking Petra had been. Yazid sat beside me and smiled. I was glad to have him close. We hadn't spoken much during the visit; he had led the group, while I stayed near the back. Using my exhaustion as an excuse, I rested my head on his shoulder.

We left that extraordinary place behind and made our way to a Bedouin camp in the Wadi Rum desert, where we would spend the night. We drove down narrow secondary roads that seemed to disappear into the sand. The darkness was complete—

no other cars in sight. We passed signs for various camps until we finally reached ours. It wasn't very big, but it felt welcoming. Traditional Bedouin tents formed a semicircle around a central area covered in carpets. At the center, a fire pit was surrounded by low tables and sofas. Families and other groups were already enjoying the evening, with live music playing and hookah being passed around. Once again, we were the last to arrive.

Our hosts were waiting for us with dinner already prepared: lamb cooked Bedouin-style, slow-roasted for hours in an underground oven buried in the sand. Too hungry to shower, we went straight to the dining area. Within minutes, large platters of steaming lamb, vegetables, and rice covered the table. We barely spoke as we ate, our fatigue was evident, and the food was delicious.

After dinner, we split into tents: girls on one side, boys on the other. I would be sharing with Sofía. After a quick shower, feeling clean and refreshed, we regrouped around the fire, not for warmth, but for its cozy glow. We sipped black tea with mint and shared several hookahs. I glanced up at the sky and saw a full moon overhead, it coincided with the summer solstice. It was, without a doubt, a special night.

"This night is perfect! What if we sleep out here on the sofas?" Sofía suggested cheerfully.

"Great idea!" Harita and Mark, one of the American students, replied in unison.

Sofía was well liked in the group, and her ideas were usually met with eager approval. The sofas were wide enough for two people to lie down comfortably. Excited, we went to get our pillows. Without knowing why, or perhaps knowing exactly why, Yazid placed his pillow next to mine. Lying down, our heads almost touched. I felt a rush of nerves. We said goodnight to each other, and slowly, the conversation faded into silence.

After a while, just as sleep began to pull me in, I felt Yazid's hand brush gently across my cheek. I flinched, then leaned into his touch. Once again, I found myself on uncertain ground. I thought of Daniel, and guilt returned, but I reminded myself that I was here because he had chosen not to come. That thought quieted the inner conflict. Yazid's hand moved down my neck and into my hair. My heart beat faster. With his hand, he turned my face toward his. His face was much closer than I remembered before closing my eyes. Then his lips met mine, soft and gentle.

"Lola…" he whispered, kissing me again. "You have no idea how long I've been waiting for this moment. Come with me."

He sat up quietly and, after making sure everyone else was asleep, took my hand. We slipped away into a corner of the common area, hidden in the moonlight's shadow. From a timid kiss, we moved to embraces, to caresses, and then to deeper, more passionate kisses. That night, we crossed a line, one that would bring consequences neither of us could have foreseen.

Beneath the full moon, we gave in to the tension between us, finally uncovering the truth of a desire we could no longer hide. We lost all sense of time in a blur of kisses and caresses, both of us consumed by longing. He spoke softly about the first day we met, how much he liked my accent, my shyness, my black dress and denim jacket, the shape of my eyes, and the waves in my hair.

He held me in a way no one ever had, tenderly and longingly, as if he had missed me for a lifetime.

There was something deeply romantic in the way he touched me, gentle, careful, and yet somehow able to ignite every part of me. Yazid was irresistible. Maybe it was the exotic air about him, or the quiet mystery that surrounded him. He called me *habibti*, which means "my love" in Arabic. He wasn't afraid to express how he felt, and I loved that. We curled up together on one of the cushioned benches in the common area, and sleep found us slowly. Before anyone else woke up, I slipped back to the tent I'd been assigned, as if I'd spent the whole night there.

The next day, we pretended nothing had happened, exchanging glances in silence, a private game that would last until the end of the trip. Maybe it was the desert's spell, or the look in his eyes, but my mind felt like it was somewhere else entirely.

That morning, after breakfast and packing up our things, we went on a desert tour with the Bedouins in 4x4 trucks. Wadi Rum looked like Mars, with its orange sands and reddish rocks in strange shapes. The Bedouins had a unique aesthetic, long dark hair, and eyes lined with black kohl. We stopped at a tent for tourists, where they sold clothes and cosmetics and offered camel rides. They lined our eyes with kohl, invited us to drink tea, and even offered marijuana. Yazid and I exchanged knowing smiles, always looking for an excuse to touch, a brush of the arm, a gentle tap on the shoulder to say something trivial. We were like two kids in on a secret.

From Wadi Rum, we headed to Aqaba to visit the Red Sea and go snorkeling. The beach felt nothing like the ones back in Spain, not because of the sea or the sand, but because of what people were wearing. Most of the women were fully covered, while the men wore shorts and t-shirts. It felt strange to me, and unfair. We boarded a glass-bottom boat that gave us a short tour of the coastline and its sea life. The water was dark, and we could barely see the bottom. What I remember most from that part of the day is Yazid gently running his fingers along my arm when no one was watching, and how we swam side by side, playing with our legs beneath the surface, pretending nothing was out of the ordinary.

After that weekend, I lost control of the situation. Our feelings didn't stop growing, deeper and more intense. I barely thought about the consequences, and even less about how Daniel would feel if he ever found out. I pushed him out of my mind and postponed that internal conversation, choosing instead to live in the present, with Yazid. I knew I was being selfish, but I convinced myself that as long as Daniel never knew, nothing would change. As long as it remained a secret, there would be no consequences.

5

As the days went by, Yazid and I grew closer and closer. To avoid complications, we decided to keep our relationship a secret. He didn't want the other Jordanians finding out and turning it into gossip, and I felt guilty for being unfaithful to Daniel, I didn't want anyone judging me either. Around others, we pretended to be just friends, but we always found an excuse to sneak off alone. Keeping it secret only made the tension stronger, made us crave each other more. We both lived for those moments.

Sometimes we managed to meet up in private, but most of our alone time came during drives to or from group gatherings. Yazid would take the longest route possible, full of stoplights. Whenever he could, he'd rest his hand on my thigh, and at red lights, he'd look at me and smile. We never kissed in public, kissing was considered private, even taboo. Yazid liked smoking weed, and if the streets were quiet enough, he'd light a joint while driving and pass it to me on the way to my place. A few puffs in, I'd feel like I was floating, and the sensation of his hand on my leg became almost otherworldly. When we reached my street, he'd pull into a side alley, turn off the headlights, and we'd devour each other in the dark. More than once, things got too heated, and we were left wanting more, yet we never crossed that line.

I loved getting lost in his black eyes, in that deep, unreadable gaze. The more time we spent together, the more I liked him. Behind his outgoing charm and easy smile, there was someone private, someone with a rich inner world. Little by little, he opened up to me, and I learned that his life had been more complex than I had imagined.

Yazid wasn't Jordanian, he was Palestinian, like many of the other students. His roots were in a region of olive groves in the north, near the city of Haifa and not far from the Mediterranean. From the way he described it, I pictured something like the landscapes of southern Spain. His parents had fled after getting married, forced out by the Israeli occupation, and settled in Riyadh, Saudi Arabia. His father was an engineer and his mother a doctor, so finding work wasn't hard. His father started a construction company during the oil boom and eventually expanded it to Jordan, taking advantage of the fact that his children were studying there—and that Amman was constantly growing as more people arrived fleeing conflict in neighboring countries.

Yazid had grown up in Riyadh with his four siblings. After finishing high school, he moved to Amman to study medicine.

All of his siblings, except the youngest, had also ended up studying in Jordan. His oldest sister was married and lived with her husband, also a doctor, in one of the most upscale neighborhoods in Amman. His youngest sister, twenty-one like me, was studying medicine in Irbid, Jordan's second-largest city. His older brother was a dentist and also lived in Amman. Since neither of them was married, they shared an apartment and got along well. They made a great team, helping each other with daily life and working together in the family business. When their father had a project in Amman, Yazid and his brother acted as site supervisors, coordinating workers and solving problems on-site. That surprised me. In Spain, it would be almost unthinkable for a medical student to juggle their studies with a second job, especially something so unrelated, like managing construction. But everything came at a cost. He barely had time for anything outside of studying and the family business. That made it all the more impressive that he still found time to see me and hang out with the other students.

One afternoon, in the middle of the week, Yazid came to pick me up after my hospital rotation. He had parked in double file and was leaning against the side of the car. The sun was blazing on his face, but he didn't seem to care. He smiled, and his smile grew wider when he saw me approaching. He was wearing a white shirt and navy-blue trousers. Elegant and confident, as always. I, on the other hand, was still in my white coat, wearing loose pants and a striped shirt. The plan had come together at the last minute, and I hadn't had time to dress up.

"You look great in that white coat. I'm so happy to see you again," he said with a smile. "How are you?"

"Thanks," I replied shyly. "Have you been waiting long? It's so hot today." We kept our distance, avoiding any hugs or physical contact.

"Don't worry, just ten minutes." He opened the door and motioned for me to get in.

"Ten minutes in this heat is a lot," I said, waiting for him to sit down before continuing. "So, where are we going?"

"I'm dying to kiss you," he said. No one could see or hear us now, and he placed his hand on my thigh.

"Yazid…" I smiled, lowering my gaze to where his hand rested.

"I can't help it," he said, starting the engine. "I want to take you somewhere beautiful."

Yazid had a way with words. Maybe it was his accent, or maybe it was just him, but there was something magnetic about his voice. We both held back our urge to kiss. It was broad daylight, and someone could see us.

That afternoon, Yazid took me to a place that was very special to him: the King Abdullah Mosque, one of the most beautiful and iconic landmarks in Amman. It was also known as the Blue Mosque because of its turquoise dome. I had seen pictures before, but in person, it was even more striking. It stood in the heart of the city, and just across from it was an Orthodox Christian church, a symbol of the harmony that exists in Jordan between Muslims and Christians. When we arrived, we dressed in black cloaks called *abayas*. Soon after, we had to separate to enter the prayer halls, since in Islam, men and women pray in different spaces. We agreed to meet up again in half an hour.

Like any other worshipper, I walked silently into the women's prayer hall. Since it wasn't time for *salat*, or prayer, the space was nearly empty, and a sense of calm lingered in every corner. Sunlight filtered through the stained-glass windows, casting color across the walls. A deep red carpet covered the floor, soft under my bare feet, muffling each step. The silence of the room gave me space to reflect on everything that had happened that month. A wave of guilt came over me as I thought of Daniel, but it was already too late for regret. The damage was done, and I had long since lost control of my feelings for Yazid.

After visiting the mosque, Yazid took me for a stroll through Downtown. He knew how much I loved sweets and wanted me to try the most famous Jordanian dessert: *knaafeh*, a warm pastry filled with cheese. He brought me to one of the city's most traditional bakeries, and on top of that, he bought a box of *baklava*, another popular treat, insisting I had to try it too. It was far too much sugar, but it was all so good we didn't leave a single bite behind.

By the time we finished devouring more dessert than we should have, we both felt sluggish. Neither of us wanted to go anywhere else, and for the first time, Yazid suggested we go to his place. Though we didn't say it aloud, we were both eager for that intimacy, and the timing was perfect. His house was only fifteen minutes away, and his brother would be working late at the clinic. The place would be empty, and we'd have a couple of hours all to ourselves.

Yazid lived in a quiet neighborhood of single-family homes. His was a one-story house built above a garage, and we had to climb a set of stairs to get in. The decor was simple and functional, everything tidy and in its place. The furniture had a traditional Arabic style, but it was clear neither he nor his brother cared much for aesthetics or details. He showed me around, saving his bedroom for last.

The blinds were halfway down, casting a soft dimness over the room. He hugged me and then kissed me deeply. Taking my hand, he led me to the bed. My heart raced. I had fantasized about this moment many nights, but I hadn't expected it to happen that afternoon. We collapsed onto the bed and lost ourselves in kisses and caresses. Yazid slowly began undressing me, and I him, with no rush. We had never gone this far before, and everything felt more intense.

"Lola," he whispered in my ear, "I've never been with anyone like this before. I'm a little embarrassed to say it, but I think you should know."

"It's okay," I whispered back, kissing his neck. "You're here with me now." I tried to put him at ease.

Even though it wasn't my first time, it felt like discovering something new. Everything was heightened, like I was in another dimension. With him, nothing else existed. That afternoon, we erased the space that once stood between us, and I felt closer to him than ever. Our bond kept deepening. I was falling in love.

In the days that followed, I distanced myself from Daniel even more. I didn't want to talk to him, didn't want to keep pretending. I hated lying, but I didn't have the courage to tell him what was happening in Jordan. Thankfully, he was still somewhere in the middle of the Atlantic Ocean, with patchy, unreliable reception. That lack of connection helped hide the truth, and kept him from suspecting anything. It also helped me focus completely on Yazid, letting our feelings grow stronger by the day.

6

*It was barely five in the morning, and the first rays of sunlight were lighting up the room. The window was open, and the call to prayer woke me. The solemn voice of the imam pierced the stillness of dawn. For many, it served as their alarm clock, and that morning, it was mine too. I didn't understand the words, but hearing them brought me peace. Yazid was still asleep. I reached for his hands and pulled them toward me.

The room was small and impersonal, the product of an improvised décor, like the rest of the house. There was only a bed beneath the window and a desk facing it. On the two remaining walls stood bookshelves packed with textbooks. That was about it. I pictured his long nights studying there under the glow of his desk lamp, and the moments between, kneeling on the red prayer rug folded neatly in the corner. I found myself wondering: what direction was Mecca from this room? Had he used a compass the first time to figure it out? And what if he prayed facing the wrong way, would it still count?

Though we were both studying medicine, our experiences couldn't have been more different. I had studied at home, with my parents' constant support and the comfort it brought. My only real worries had been passing exams, going out with friends, and spending time with Daniel. Yazid, on the other hand, lived far from his parents, shared an apartment with his brother, and had no one waiting at home with a hot meal on the table. On top of that, he helped run his father's construction business. And yet he made it all seem effortless. I admired him deeply for that.

Yazid stirred and pulled me into an embrace, pressing a kiss to my neck that snapped me out of my thoughts. He noticed my distant stare and asked what I was thinking about. I didn't know how to answer, so I kissed him instead. It was my last day in Amman, and we only had a few hours left before my flight. Looking back, I was surprised by how quickly the days had flown by. Even more surprising was how deeply I'd fallen for him, how this had turned into something much more than a summer romance.

Yazid cared for me like no one ever had. His way of loving was unlike anything I'd known. With him, I felt seen, understood, safe. Whatever I needed, whether I said it out loud or not, he sensed it and responded. In a way, he was the man who best cared for the little girl I still carried inside. He made me feel special, irreplaceable, one of a kind. He had opened every door to me: his home, his privacy, his thoughts, and his heart. In time, I would come to understand what that meant for him. Deep down, he also expected full transparency from me, that I would match his openness, meet all his needs, and reflect his emotional investment. That was something I never quite managed to do. I was used to a very different kind of relationship, one like I'd had with Daniel: independent and free.Sometimes I couldn't help but compare them, and the truth was, they were opposites in almost every way. Maybe that polarity was what made Yazid so irresistible. He filled all the spaces Daniel never could. Yazid was affectionate, attentive, always eager to spend time with me. He treated me like a queen, and he meant it. He brought me into his world with ease. He introduced me to his brother, his friends, making our time together feel natural. I was the center of everything for him, and the way he looked at me, as if the answers to all his questions were in my eyes, made me melt.

Daniel, on the other hand, had always been defined by his independence and detachment. He never introduced me to his friends, let alone his family. Our relationship had always been on-and-off, full of gaps and lacking commitment. We could go days without seeing each other, even though we lived just five minutes apart. I'll admit, that kind of distance had its advantages. It never held me back, never stifled me. I had space to grow on my own. But all that space also left room for other people, for other possibilities to walk in. I'm not trying to excuse myself, but that openness probably made what happened with Yazid easier to fall into.

Their personalities were night and day. Daniel was a dreamer, abstract, free of fixed values, and untethered to the world. He lost himself in thought and the philosophy of perspective. For him, there were no good people or bad people, just circumstances. He believed in personal freedom above all and used to tell me we were each free to do as we wished, that we should be honest with our desires, not obligated by someone else's. Yazid, by contrast, saw the world in black and white. He had clearly defined values, honesty and communication chief among them. To him, there was only one right way, one moral line between good and bad. Religiously, they were just as different. Daniel was not a believer. Yazid was a practicing Muslim, though to be fair, not particularly strict. He had his flexible moments, sometimes a bit selectively so, which I found slightly unsettling.

The truth is, I was more like Daniel, and the gap between Yazid's world and mine was vast. But I didn't want to see that then. I wasn't ready to face it.

As we lay in bed together, Yazid finally brought up a conversation we had both been avoiding.

"Lola, I want to see you again. I know this started off as something casual, and I know you have things to sort out in Gijón, but I've been thinking, why don't you stay with me for the rest of the summer? We could take the US residency prep course together," he said, gently running his hand over my shoulder.

"I'd love to," I replied, not really knowing what else to say. The question had caught me off guard. "But I have no idea how the residency process works there, and my English still needs a lot of work."

"Whatever you want…" he said, clearly disappointed. "But we could do it together. We could build a future."

I wasn't ready for that kind of proposition. The thought of it made my head spin. As much as I enjoyed being with him, part of me longed for the sea breeze and the freedom of my city, the bike rides, the light drizzle, the cloudy skies. I missed coffee with my friends, lazy afternoons on the couch with my mom, siesta hours, mountain hikes with my dad and sister. I didn't want to stay in Jordan for the rest of the summer. All these reasons ran through my head, but I had the feeling he wouldn't understand. He would take it as a rejection. Maybe because he was opening a door to a future together, and I didn't have a clear idea of what I wanted at all.

Without a word, he gave me a soft kiss. His expression weighed down, maybe accepting the truth neither of us could say out loud: that in just a few hours, something vast would come between us.

The day flew by, and soon it was time to head to the airport. Before we left, we lay down together on the bed, still unmade, sheets in one corner, pillows in another, the two of us in the middle. The light of the sunset filtered through the slats of the half-closed blinds, casting ellipses across the wall. In the stillness of the afternoon, the final call to prayer echoed through the city, my last one before leaving. Yazid knew I loved hearing it, so he opened the window so the sound would reach us better.

Facing each other, hand in hand, feet entwined, we stared into one another's eyes in silence.

"Lola, you were the last thing I ever expected this summer," he said, burying his face in my chest. "I don't know what I'll do when you're gone."

"Everything will be okay," I said, trying to be the strong one. I didn't want to lose control.

"My *habibti*. We'll see each other soon. You know full moons have your name now."

We wrapped each other in a long embrace. The sadness clung to me and would stay with me for weeks. Yazid had been both a surprise and a blessing in my life. I was going to miss him terribly.

We set off for the airport. As I walked down the stairs of his house, I turned around one last time to say goodbye to the place that had become our refuge. Yazid followed, dragging my suitcase, and smiled when our eyes met.

In the car, Amr Diab was playing, and the night breeze came in through the windows. Yazid held my hand whenever he wasn't shifting gears, humming along softly to the music. I didn't know what to say to fill the silence, so I said nothing, just held his hand and focused on the warmth of his skin.

So much had changed in just one month. The Lola who was leaving that place was nothing like the one who had arrived in early June. We shared one last kiss in the parking lot, hidden between cars, our goodbye done as privately as it had to be. He walked me to the gate, stretching our final moments together for as long as we could.

Then came the airport announcement: the flight to Madrid was boarding. I had to go.

I stole a kiss in the middle of the crowd. He hesitated, but couldn't resist. A few people turned to look, but we didn't care. I knew kissing in public was frowned upon, but I didn't know when I'd get the chance again. I couldn't let that moment slip away.

I held him tightly, until I felt like I couldn't get any closer. He kissed my forehead. I kissed the back of his hand in return, a gesture of love and respect. Then I turned and slipped into the crowd. Just before rounding the corner to the boarding gate, I looked back.

He was still there, eyes locked on me. With a soft smile and a wave, he said goodbye. I couldn't hold back the tears. Was I making a mistake by leaving?

7

July 18, 2013

Gijón, Asturias, Spain

I got home and pretended my story with Yazid had never happened. The first few days were confusing, I felt numb, and without him, I was hollow. I had decided to keep what happened between us to myself. I didn't know how to begin explaining it, or even how to make sense of it aloud. I feared people's reactions, especially judgment from my sister, my friends, or my parents. This wasn't an easy story to digest. First, I'd cheated on Daniel. Then, I'd fallen in love with an Arab, a Muslim. There was nothing wrong with that last part, of course, but truthfully, television and the stories people tell about the Middle East didn't help much. They were full of prejudice and distorted ideas. In Spain, many believed that Arab men gave women no freedom, that women were treated like property. That all Arab men were misogynists. That polygamy was just part of marriage.

Because of all this, I saw the situation as incredibly complicated. I knew the first reaction would be to judge me for cheating, and the second, to worry. Neither would be good. I'd have to explain too much and face stares full of assumptions. Or maybe I was just imagining all that. But those were the scenarios running through my mind. They would also worry about me, about the heartbreak of loving someone from afar, and worse, across a cultural divide, with all the complications that might bring. Once they processed everything, maybe that's what would trouble them most. We've all heard at least one of those tragic love stories between East and West, usually involving abuse, betrayal, kidnapped children during a summer trip, broken families, shattered hearts. I was being overly dramatic, spiraling into a negative loop, but I knew those thoughts would at least cross my family's minds. Fear feeds on the unknown.

So I kept it all in, my heart and my conscience caught in limbo, waiting silently for the moment and the courage to face it all. I also avoided speaking to Daniel. I was relieved he was still away on his sea voyage. His absence gave me time to process everything and better understand myself. But in just a few days, he'd be back. Then we'd see each other again, and sooner or later, we'd have to talk.

Meanwhile, I couldn't stop thinking about Yazid. I missed him deeply and wondered if he was thinking of me, of us. He'd never asked much about my relationship with Daniel, but I sensed it weighed on his mind. I knew that cheating on Daniel had triggered a deep sense of mistrust in Yazid, and that in silence, he tormented himself. During our time together in

Jordan, he would often hold my hand in public, maybe subconsciously marking territory, trying to tell the world I was his. But now, ten thousand kilometers away, he couldn't, and didn't have the right to. I knew this distance must be hard for him, too.

Several days later, Daniel came back. He hadn't slept on the trip home, but excited to be back and eager to see me, he insisted we meet that same afternoon despite being exhausted. He came to pick me up and we met at the gate of my apartment complex. He still hadn't met my parents, and had made it clear many times that he preferred it that way. All morning, I'd been a bundle of nerves, wondering whether I'd be able to tell him the truth. He had no idea what was coming.

It was four in the afternoon, siesta time at my house, when he called to say he was outside. It was a perfect summer day: clear blue skies, no clouds, no wind. The streets were quiet, almost no cars passing by. The city was at rest. I walked down the short slope from my building to the gate. With every step, my heart pounded faster. I took a deep breath. As I stepped outside, there he was.

Daniel was deeply tanned, his beard and curls messy, wearing a white T-shirt and brown shorts with beige sneakers. His mint green bicycle leaned against the wall. A huge smile lit up his face and he ran over to hug me.

I'd be lying if I said I wasn't happy to see him. Even with Yazid's sudden place in my life, Daniel still meant something to me. I still cared deeply about him.

"Baby, you have no idea how much I've missed you. The trip on the ship was incredible, but God, I couldn't wait to see you again!" He kissed me on the lips. "I've done a lot of thinking these past few days." He pulled me close again. "I should mention, you look amazing."

"I missed you too," I said, burying my face in his chest, unsure of what else to say.

Even though I was glad to see him, our reunion confirmed what I had feared, my feelings for him had changed. Now, as he held me, it just didn't feel the same. I'd let him down, let us down, and what I'd done had damaged our relationship for good. I couldn't stop thinking about how badly I'd treated him, and how little he deserved it. All the guilt I hadn't allowed myself to feel came crashing down, settling over me like a storm cloud. I felt disgusted with myself. Thankfully, Daniel couldn't hear my thoughts.

He kissed me again, and I, filled with nothing but guilt and uncertainty, just went along.

"Lola, I have an idea. Want to ride our bikes downtown and go to the Elogio del Horizonte? We could grab a drink around there," he said, smiling as he brushed my cheek. He was brimming with joy.

"Sure! I'll go get my bike. Give me five minutes," I replied, already wondering when the right moment would come to tell him the truth.

I pushed back the guilt as I walked back to my house to grab my bike. Maybe the ocean breeze would help me find the words

I was missing. Maybe this afternoon I'd finally find the courage to tell him everything.

We rode across the city until we reached the beach. We took the Schulz Avenue, a road reserved for buses and taxis, which at that hour was completely empty. We weren't wearing helmets, and we didn't rush. We rode side by side, enjoying the calm of having the street to ourselves. Daniel was in high spirits, telling me stories from his time on the ship, while I listened in silence. He talked about how strange it felt to touch solid ground after days at sea, about sunrises and sunsets that painted everything in deep reds, the camaraderie with the crew, and the simplicity of life on a boat. His face lit up with every memory. He looked incredibly attractive. His strong jawline, sharp nose, tousled curls, and athletic frame gave him the look of a Greek god. The more time I spent with him, the more I realized how much I had missed his presence.

That's when I understood it wasn't going to be easy to end things with him. Besides, Gijón was so closely tied to him, and I knew life would be simpler if I stayed with Daniel, in my hometown, in my culture. I enjoyed being with him, our bike rides, our conversations. I was in love with Yazid, but now that Daniel was in front of me, my feelings were all mixed up.

We biked through the city center until we reached Cimadevilla, Gijón's oldest neighborhood. We rode uphill to the Elogio del Horizonte, a sculpture in a park with stunning views of the city and the sea. Despite being on the coast and atop a hill, there was barely any wind. Locals and tourists alike strolled by, enjoying the view. From there, facing the ocean, we could see San

Lorenzo Beach to the right, and the marina to the left. The city itself stretched behind us, with its mix of buildings and, beyond that, green hills and mountains.

We sat on one of our favorite benches, looking out to sea. Daniel wrapped his arm around me and pulled me close. He had always been affectionate. He radiated peace and had this incredible ability to stay in a good mood and see the bright side of everything. His emotional stability rose above life's daily noise. He always said he'd reached that point thanks to meditation and learning to really listen to himself.

That afternoon, Daniel was glowing, partly from being back, partly from seeing me again. He was happy to be with me, to enjoy our time together. But my mind was elsewhere. I kept going over and over how to tell him what had happened in Jordan. Every silence felt like the perfect opening to tell the truth... but I never managed to say it. I just kept quiet. And so, after telling me all about his adventures, he noticed something was off. I hadn't really shared anything about my time in Jordan.

"Baby, what's going on?" he asked. "It feels like your head is somewhere else. Tell me."

"No... nothing's wrong... I think I'm just tired," I said, brushing it off with a kiss on the cheek and resting my head on his chest.

I couldn't do it. I didn't have the strength or the words. I told myself it would be better to wait a couple of days, that I'd find the right moment. I tried to silence the little voice inside that kept telling me this wasn't right, that I needed to be honest with him soon, that I couldn't keep pretending for much longer.

Luckily, that afternoon, Daniel didn't push. That's just how he was, calm and thoughtful. He trusted me completely, and also trusted himself. He didn't insist.

Those next few days were strange. While I tried to sort out what I should do and how to do it, I kept talking to Yazid in secret and avoided Daniel. The situation became unbearable. Daniel wasn't stupid, he had already sensed my distance. In the end, I had no choice but to face reality. No more waiting for the perfect setting I'd imagined. One night, in his bedroom, fed up with my behavior, while we lay in bed, he brought it up.

"Lola," he said. He only ever used my full name when things were serious. "Since you came back from Jordan, you've been distant. It feels like you treat me more like a friend than your boyfriend. Tell me… what's going on?"

"I'm sorry. I know I should've told you sooner…" I sighed and stared up at the ceiling, avoiding his eyes. "I met someone in Jordan and… I don't know, it just spiraled."

"Okay," he cut in, sitting up in bed. "Why didn't you tell me earlier?" His expression was full of disappointment.

"I'm really, really sorry. It started out as something small, something playful… and then I got in over my head."

He lowered his gaze. We talked for a long time. He didn't ask for many details, he was too hurt. He blamed himself for not going on the trip with me. He thought that maybe, if he hadn't left me on my own, none of this would've happened. A tear slid down his cheek and landed on his knee, where his elbows were resting. He covered his face, trying to hide his emotions.

"This really hurts, but I get it. What a shame," he said, his voice thick with pain. "I guess we're not a couple anymore. Maybe we never really were…"

"I'm sorry. I never meant to hurt you," I said, my voice cracking.

"It's already done. I wish you the best," he said, trying to keep himself composed. "I imagine it can't be easy for you either, falling for someone who lives so far away and comes from such a different world. Take care of yourself."

Head down, he walked me to the door. We didn't exchange another look. I walked out and down the stairs of his building, a place where we had shared so many good times. I got home after midnight, and even though I tried not to make any noise, my mom, always a light sleeper, heard me come in. The next morning, when she saw me, she understood something had happened with Daniel. She didn't ask any questions. She just hugged me.

The days that followed were bleak. Guilt weighed me down, and I couldn't stop thinking about our conversation, his heartbreak lingered in my mind. I felt like I had torn his heart in half, and I couldn't forgive myself. Daniel had been my first boyfriend, the one who'd taught me what love was supposed to feel like. I owed him so much. We had spent our early university years together, and now that he was gone, every memory resurfaced with renewed force.

His reaction stayed with me. The empathy he showed, the way he tried to understand me, even after my betrayal and lack of respect, had taught me a powerful lesson. He had cared for me, and for the difficulty of falling in love across distances. In his quiet way, Daniel had shown me what real love looks like.

And I couldn't help but feel I had made a mistake. That I hadn't lived up to him. That for Yazid, who might end up being nothing more than a summer romance, I had lost someone truly irreplaceable.

8

Remorse and doubt stayed with me for weeks. For several days, I ignored my phone, dodging Yazid's calls. I felt terrible about what had happened with Daniel—and about myself. I needed time to think, and I kept wondering if being alone in such a distant country had made me more vulnerable. Maybe I'd mistaken the sense of safety and protection I felt with Yazid for love. My mind wouldn't stop searching for explanations, constantly analyzing every detail and trying to untangle my emotions.

Guilt lingered too, and I couldn't get used to the silence between Daniel and me. I knew it was for the best, but it still felt strange not to hear from him. Every time I walked down his street, I'd glance up at his window. If I saw a light on, I'd picture him lying in bed with his laptop, staring at the blank wall. What had once been a loving nest had become just another room in an unfamiliar building. Yet amid my turmoil, I found myself thinking about my summer in Amman.

After a few days of avoiding Yazid, I began to answer his calls again. He'd given me space and hadn't pressured me, but he sensed something was wrong and asked me directly, no beating around the bush. He had a right to know; after all, even if our relationship was undefined, it was still long-distance. I felt relieved when he brought it up. I told him I'd spoken with Daniel and that we were over. Yazid didn't ask any more questions, but I heard relief in his tone.

From that moment on, our conversations grew more intense, perhaps because we missed each other more, or because by confiding in him, I'd given him the confidence to take a chance on us. I let myself get carried away every time I heard his voice, though sometimes I felt a sense of vertigo when I thought about our situation. I had no idea where our story would lead. Yazid remained a secret in my life, neither my family nor my friends had any clue what was happening in my head and my heart.

Amid all that uncertainty, I still hadn't processed what had happened with Daniel. Everything in Gijón reminded me of him. And yet, even as my emotions swirled, my thoughts often drifted back to Yazid.

Despite the distance, my relationship with Yazid advanced almost without my realizing it. What began as mutual attraction and curiosity was slowly evolving into something real and serious. Though we'd agreed to carry on with our lives, we both fantasized about being together again. We talked every day and

70

missed each other more with each call. Maybe I was vulnerable, but I found comfort in his voice.

Talking to him became a necessity. Time would slip away, and we'd end up chatting until the early hours without noticing. I'd wait for nightfall, when everyone else was asleep, then sneak out to the terrace. Wrapped in a blanket, I'd lie on the cold floor, listening to his voice and gazing at the sky, mistaking the moon for his smile.

The secret didn't last long. One night, my sister woke up and found me on the terrace, speaking English. She said nothing then, but the next day her probing questions forced me to confess. At first, she was upset that I'd kept my relationship with Yazid hidden, but she soon understood how complicated things had been and calmed down. I told her everything: the night we met, our first kiss, our days in Amman, the goodbye at the airport... I was surprised to realize I missed him even more as I relived those moments.

My sister, Sara, and I were twins, identical on the outside but very different on the inside. Well, no longer identical: my face had grown longer, and our mannerisms, styles, and personalities had diverged. Anyone paying attention could tell us apart. She was the responsible one: a rule-follower, rational and conventional. Sometimes she took on the role of the older sister, and this was definitely one of those times.

Sara bombarded me with questions, flooding my mind with doubts about Yazid, our future, and the kind of influence he might have on my life. Until then, I hadn't considered the consequences, and she brought me crashing down from the cloud I'd been floating on since I returned from Jordan. As I told my story, everything took on a different tone, and reality hit me hard.

After that conversation, I began to reevaluate my situation with Yazid and search for answers to the questions I knew I'd eventually face. For now, all we had were phone calls, but the emotions were powerful, and I couldn't forget everything we'd shared in Jordan. I started imagining a future with him, and how I might make it real.

I pictured Yazid visiting, or perhaps vacationing here, but never living in Spain, and certainly not fitting into my hometown, which was rather closed-minded and homogeneous. I couldn't ignore the suspicion that Spanish society still harbored toward the Middle East, Arabs, and Muslims, fueled by media coverage and the atrocities committed by Islamist extremists in the West.

Moreover, the version of history we learned in school didn't portray Muslims favorably, mostly as invaders of Al-Andalus. That image still lingers in our collective subconscious. I couldn't imagine Yazid being accepted in Gijón. Maybe in a big city like Madrid or Barcelona it would be easier… And on top of that, he didn't speak Spanish, so communication would be limited.

As for me, I couldn't picture myself living in Amman either. Their culture was so different from ours, and there were countless everyday things I still didn't understand. On top of that, I had deeply missed the freedom of my own city: the freedom to ride a bike, to dress and act however I wanted, to read signs, and, most importantly, to understand people. I knew that would always be a challenge in Amman. I'd lose my voice and my freedom, and I'd have to learn Arabic just to communicate. Not to mention my already limited English, realistically, it just wasn't a viable option.

Maybe I was getting ahead of myself with all these hypothetical scenarios and premature conclusions. Maybe, in the end, our relationship would only last a few months of phone calls. The simplest thing, both short- and long-term, would be for it to remain a summer romance. But I couldn't forget those moments we shared, and the idea of seeing him again, of spending even one more minute with him, made me smile.

I got used to carrying my phone everywhere, it was the only way to feel close to him, to keep us connected. The line between missing him and being obsessed wasn't all that clear. From the outside, anyone would've seen the situation as irrational, but I didn't care. I had eyes only for him. Our conversations gave us time to talk about everything: the past, the present, our day-to-day lives, trivial things like our favorite foods, and deeper topics like religion and our values. Each morning, I'd grab my phone almost reflexively to read his good morning messages, they became my dose of caffeine.

As we got to know each other better, we compared our ideas and perspectives. Sometimes they aligned, but most of the time, they were different. Yazid made me rethink so many things I'd always done on autopilot and never questioned. He, on the other hand, measured his time almost to the second and didn't waste a minute. His mind was highly structured, and time was his most valuable resource.

Even though the phone helped us stay close, it soon wasn't enough. At night, when I turned off the lights, dreams turned his absence into nightmares. We both longed for each other, and our conversations always ended with the fantasy of being reunited. We didn't have a shared plan for the future, but little by little, we started planning how we might see each other again. The easiest option was for me to go back to Jordan. Even though I was in my fifth year of medical school, my schedule was better and more flexible than his. Yazid was involved in one of his father's projects and couldn't leave the city. Besides, my visa cost just twenty Jordanian dinars, with no bureaucracy, no extra documents. If he wanted to come to Spain, he'd have to go to the embassy, meet several requirements… it would take much longer.

So, for all those reasons, we decided I would go in November, when I could miss a few university days without being penalized. I had some money saved up for the ticket, and he would take care of the other expenses. The hardest part was telling my parents.

I chose a sunny day, sun always helps, to break the news. I waited until siesta time, one of the few moments when both of my parents were home and relaxed. My dad was lying on the sofa with his legs up, and my mom, wrapped in a blanket, was napping on the other couch. I sat down in the armchair beside them to watch TV while I waited for them to wake up. Nervous, with my heart in my throat, I sat through the end of the animal documentaries on Channel Two, a classic in our house. My mom seemed a bit surprised to see me there after four o'clock.

74

"Don't you have studying to do, Lola?" she asked. The semester had barely started, but she was already worried about my exams.

"I need to tell you something," I said, eyes still fixed on the screen.

"Is it about a boy? Do you have a boyfriend?" she asked, her motherly intuition kicking in as she sat up and opened her eyes.

"Sometimes I think you can read my mind," I said with a playful smile, trying to hide my nerves. "Yeah, I do."

My dad was still stretching and not fully paying attention. I explained the situation as best I could and told them my story with Yazid. My mother's eyes widened, and a crease formed between her brows. She went quiet for a few minutes, as if searching for a solution. My father, meanwhile, frowned and said:

"You know we come from very different cultures." He sighed, and after a long, tense pause, he added, "They see you like we used to see Swedish girls in the seventies, modern, liberal… fine for a fling, but not for commitment."

My dad kept going along that line, and I tried to tune him out. My mom, more empathetic, seemed to understand me in some way, but her comments revealed a mindset not so different from my dad's. As I had feared, they had a very narrow view of the Middle East, and their imaginations jumped to the worst-case scenarios.

We spent a long time talking in the living room. My mom recalled news stories about broken relationships and ruined families, about women killed by their Arab partners, about children abducted by their fathers during summer vacations... My dad, more rational but no more optimistic, emphasized the cultural differences and how life abroad was so unlike ours. He reminded me that what's considered good or bad depends entirely on the context. I suppose their reactions came from a place of protection, but that didn't make it any easier for me. The whole conversation overwhelmed me. I went to my room to study and to text Yazid about what had happened with my parents.

I thought he would take it better, but maybe I had been too candid in sharing my family's rejection of the situation. I'd be lying if I said their words didn't affect me. Some of their ideas began to take root in my mind, and suddenly, I was the one with doubts.

I guess he couldn't see things from my perspective. Instead of appreciating the effort and courage it took me to bring up something so difficult and delicate, he only saw their rejection, and my hesitation. I got upset with him, and he with me.

Despite how awkward that conversation with my parents had been, things gradually eased over the next few days. Little by little, they came to terms with the situation and began to accept it. I suppose it had been a shock for them, and they just needed time. Half-joking, my dad lamented letting me go to Jordan and peppered me with questions about Yazid: his family, his job, his background, and what our plans for the future were. That last bit made me uncomfortable, since I had no answer. My mom, on the other hand, couldn't see past the headlines and kept sharing horror stories at bedtime.

My parents' attitude didn't make things any easier, but at least they didn't oppose my trip to Jordan. It took some effort, but eventually they agreed to give me the space and freedom to make my own choices. Still, a lingering sense of distrust remained.

My father, who still disapproved of my relationship with Yazid, refused to give me a single euro for the trip. He suggested Yazid come here and even offered to host him at our house, but to me, that option seemed far more complicated. For starters, he didn't speak Spanish, so he wouldn't be able to communicate with my parents, which would be awkward. And with them around, we'd have almost no privacy. I decided to ignore the invitation and focus on making the journey myself. Besides, I was thrilled to return to that exotic country, the one that had stolen my heart.

One night, in the early hours during one of our calls, we set the final dates for my trip, and I took the last step: I bought the plane tickets. I woke up the next day thinking I'd lost my mind, but it was done. All I could think about was seeing him again.

9

November 15, 2013

Madrid, Spain

It had been four months since we said goodbye at the Amman airport. That Friday marked a turning point for both of us, the day of our long-awaited reunion had finally come. I didn't care that it was the middle of the academic term. Many would've seen it as irresponsible, but to me, the joy of seeing him again far outweighed any academic setback. I had planned around my exams and could afford to miss a few classes without harming my grades. I slipped away without telling my university friends. I trusted them, but this was too delicate to become the subject of campus gossip. Aside from my closest friends, no one even knew Yazid existed.

I got to Barajas Airport on the first bus of the morning, three hours before takeoff. "A direct flight to Amman, a direct flight into his arms," I thought, ticket in hand as I walked through security after checking my bag. I kept imagining what it would feel like to hug him again, to be by his side.

Nervous and full of anticipation, I made my way through the airport, surrounded by travelers with their own stories and destinations. I passed other young women walking alone and told myself that more than one of them was also flying toward the love of her life, that going back to Amman wasn't such a crazy idea after all.

I waited at the gate, restless, watching the clock for boarding to begin. To calm myself, I opened my cardiology notes, arrhythmias was the next topic on the syllabus. But my mind wouldn't settle. Fear, doubt, and uncertainty crept in. Was I really doing the right thing by getting on that plane? I looked up, scanning the other passengers, wondering what had brought each of them here.

Next to me sat a woman of about seventy, also traveling alone. Slender and marked by age, she wore a modest dress cinched at the waist. She spoke on the phone loudly and without concern for who might overhear. After hanging up, she noticed my notes and used them as an excuse to start a conversation. She seemed like the embodiment of every prejudice I'd ever had. The exchange quickly became personal, and she opened up about her life: her marriage to a Jordanian man, and their early divorce, brought on by culture shock and his rigidity. Probing, she asked what had brought me on this flight. I didn't give her much detail, but she saw through it and guessed right away. Then, without hesitation, she offered me a piece of advice I wouldn't forget:

"Right now, he lets you read and study," she said, twisting the cap off a water bottle, "but don't expect that to last after you're married. Your role will change, and it'll be in the home. Think hard about what you want. Passion fades. Then reality kicks in." She took a long drink, staring straight ahead.

I didn't know how to respond. I hadn't expected a conversation like that, especially not with a stranger, and especially not now, on the eve of this trip, when my nerves were already on edge. I chose to dismiss her warning. Her advice felt presumptuous, colored by her own story, which didn't have to be mine. I refused to believe that every love story with an Arab man ended in disappointment.

In fact, that conversation may have had the opposite effect. It made me even more determined to move forward, to keep discovering Yazid and the world he came from. I lost sight of her once we boarded the plane. As we began to taxi, a shiver ran through me. But my fears stayed behind on that runway. For the next five hours, between brief naps and half-hearted study, all I could think about was Yazid's smile, and what it would feel like to fall into his arms again.

We landed just after sunset. The sky was clear, the night calm. With the new moon overhead, the stars were bright. After passing through customs and collecting my suitcase, I ducked into the restroom to touch up my makeup and tidy myself as best I could. I wanted to look perfect for our reunion, perfect for him. Maybe it was fear that made me linger longer than necessary, as if some part of me was stalling the moment. My heart pounded in my throat.

I stepped through the arrivals gate and searched the crowd until I saw him, leaning against a wall directly across from the exit. Our eyes met, and his lit up instantly. His smile, wider and warmer than ever, radiated pure joy. In that instant, I knew I'd made the right choice. Forgetting everything else, I let my coat and suitcase drop and ran to him. We wrapped each other in a hug, and time stood still.

"Lola, Lola, Lola... I missed you so much," he said, holding me tight. "I'm so happy you're here."

His scent transported me back to the first night we met. We had respected the customs there and shared nothing more than a kiss on the cheek, a kiss that barely concealed how much we longed for each other.

We left the terminal and walked to the parking lot. The night was cool, and autumn was in the air. Yazid wore a black leather jacket that looked like it had been made just for him, accentuating his charm. His beard was neatly trimmed, perfectly matched with his dark, curly hair. Maybe it was just how much I'd been looking forward to seeing him, but to me, he looked even more attractive, even more handsome than he had in the summer.

We walked hand in hand to the car. On the way to Amman, we couldn't wait until we got to his place, Yazid took an exit off the highway, pulled over to the side of the road, and, with no one around, kissed me. That kiss was filled with everything we felt for each other, our secret, passionate love. I was simply happy to be beside him, finally able to hear his voice without a phone between us, without thousands of kilometers in the way.

We fell asleep in each other's arms, no clothes between us, as close as two people can be. That night was one of the sweetest I'd had in a long time. I slept deeply, feeling calm and safe in his embrace. Nothing else mattered. Our breathing synchronized in the quiet of the night. The morning found us still wrapped in each other's arms.

Those days were intense, filled with affection and passion, scattered among restaurants and long walks through Amman. To an outsider, we probably looked like a married couple. In that culture, the concept of dating barely existed, friendship often led straight to marriage. The idea of being his wife was like a fantasy, and every time I held his hand, I felt like the luckiest woman in the world.

We spent ten days together, and they were full enough to reveal so much. I got to see a bit of his daily life. One day he took me to visit the construction site he was overseeing, and I finally understood the weight of the responsibility he carried. Although he had told me he was helping his father, I had never imagined the scale of the task. He was in charge of everything, from coordinating materials with suppliers to holding meetings with architects and engineers.

I realized how preoccupied he was with his work and how much time it demanded. He had gotten involved gradually, almost without noticing, and now he barely had time to study. There were always issues: if it wasn't a delay in materials, it was employees not doing their job. His books had taken a back seat. He always said the United States was his goal, but slowly, life had started shifting his priorities. I suppose he didn't want to let his father down, he wanted to make him proud.

The days passed far too quickly. I loved waking up to the call to prayer at dawn, a sound that had become deeply tied to the city in my mind. While Yazid worked, I stayed home and tried to study. Later, he'd pick me up and we'd go out for lunch. One of my favorite restaurants was a Yemeni place near the university neighborhood where I had lived during the summer. It was simple and affordable. The most curious thing about it was that there were no utensils, you ate with bread instead. Sometimes in the afternoon we'd go to a café to study, but we always ended up goofing around like two teenagers, laughing until we couldn't focus. In the end, we never got much studying done.

The last weekend before I left, Yazid invited me to the Dead Sea. It was a popular spot for both locals and tourists. Nestled in a valley well below sea level, it was always warm, summer or winter. He picked a luxury, modern hotel with a private beach and an infinity pool overlooking the Dead Sea. On the horizon, across the water, you could see Israel, or the occupied Palestine, as Yazid called it.

The subject of Palestine was delicate. Yazid explained how the Israelis had torn his family apart, scattering them across the world. The conflict between Palestine and Israel had started after World War II, and tragically, the Palestinians had lost everything. His family was living proof of that, and I could see the sorrow in his eyes whenever he spoke about it. Before I met him, I knew very little about the conflict. I didn't fully understand the situation, but it broke my heart to see how deeply it hurt him. His brow would crease when he told me how his grandparents had been forced to flee, leaving behind their olive groves and the work of generations. That explained why his parents lived in Saudi Arabia and why he had relatives in the U.S. and the U.K.

Not wanting the Palestinian tragedy to cast a shadow over our time together, we changed the subject to lighter things. We enjoyed the hotel and its private beach. We showered and got dressed to watch the sunset. The lookout was at the top of one of the valley's mountains, and the view was breathtaking. The sun was already low, but there were still thirty minutes or so before it dipped below the horizon. The place was quiet, almost empty. I felt lucky to experience such a special moment in his company. The sunlight danced across the surface of the Dead Sea, painting the horizon in deep red tones. I had never seen anything like it.

"Do you like it?" Yazid asked, taking my hand and leading me toward the edge, where a low wall invited us to sit. "Did you know you're the first person I've ever brought here?"

"Really? Thank you... I love it," I said, squeezing his hand tightly.

"I came here just a few days after you left," he said, looking out toward the horizon, his face serious. "This is where I come when I need to think, when I need perspective." He paused. "I'm really happy you came back to Amman. I'm so glad I got to see you again."

"So am I. I have to admit, I was afraid things wouldn't work out. But these past few days have felt like a dream," I said, resting

my head on his shoulder. "I wish I could always be by your side."
I didn't filter my words, they came straight from my heart.

"Lola…" he said softly, pausing for a moment. "I want you
to be my girlfriend."

"To me, I already am," I replied. I was letting myself be
carried away by the moment, without thinking about the meaning
behind those words.

I kissed the back of his hand, our unspoken blend of
affection and respect. Surrounded by onlookers, we couldn't
share a proper kiss, so we stood embraced in silence, watching
the sun slip below the horizon and talking about us. That
moment marked a turning point in our relationship. Everything
had begun spontaneously, almost unconsciously, without
considering the consequences or the expectations quietly
forming between us. Now we were a couple: drawn together by
fierce physical attraction, tenderness, and good intentions, even
though we hardly knew one another. I didn't fully grasp his
worldview, and he didn't understand mine. We began with
blinders on, oblivious to the challenges of sustaining a
relationship divided by the Mediterranean, and even more so by
our cultural differences.

After those dreamlike days at the Dead Sea, it was time to
return to a life defined by phone calls. Those ten days felt like a
honeymoon, a time when we fell deeper in love and forged an
intimate bond. I already missed our early mornings together and
the thrill of catching his smile at random moments. This farewell
felt different from July's. This wasn't a fleeting summer romance
saying goodbye; it was two people saying, "See you later." Yet

beneath that hopeful phrase lay something heavier: a yearning for everyday closeness. Our expectations had shifted, and though we didn't voice them, we both craved the gestures and routines that would sustain our love across the miles.

We parted without knowing when we'd reunite. I clung to the hope of carving out time, and saving enough, to buy another plane ticket. Or perhaps next time Yazid would travel to Spain. But we both knew that, for the long haul, we'd have to make a real plan. Our plan.

I boarded the plane wrapped in uncertainty and fear: fear of navigating the distance again, and even greater fear of learning how to live without him by my side.

10

December 10, 2013

Gijón, Asturias, Spain

The days, and perhaps even the weeks, that followed my return proved far more grueling than I had ever anticipated. I sank back into my familiar routine: long, monotonous bus rides to and from campus, the same faces on each trip, the rumble of the engine beneath me. I did my best to bury myself in my ever-growing mountain of lecture notes and textbooks, seeking refuge in marathon study sessions. I told myself to focus on the looming cardiology exam, arrhythmias, heart blocks, EKG tracings, but only on rare occasions did my concentration hold. All too often, my mind drifted back to Amman.

I couldn't stop thinking about Yazid. Every idle moment, waiting at a bus stop, pacing the hallway outside class, played out like a highlight reel of our days together. My fingers itched to check my phone, to see if he'd messaged me, to feel that familiar buzz of his name lighting up the screen. I had no desire to engage with anyone else; every other conversation felt flat, as though my ears were tuned to a frequency only Yazid occupied.

Because of the distance, our relationship relied entirely on technology, especially on a stable internet connection. I wondered how different things might have been in another era, when lovers separated by borders had only letters or expensive, fleeting landline calls to bridge the gap.

In those pre-digital days, love across distances looked very different. Handwritten letters were fixed snapshots in time, bound by the margins of a page and sealed with a final period until the next one arrived. Phone calls were billed by the minute, never lasting more than a few precious moments. Privacy was a luxury: the family landline sat in the living room or kitchen, within earshot of everyone, and true intimacy required a solitary trip to a street-corner pay phone. Such constraints kept communication brief and infrequent, leaving daily life largely uninterrupted.

Today, with smartphones and high-speed internet, one can literally talk all day, no matter how many miles lie between you. And there I was: glued to that little screen, incapable of looking away. When not on a three-hour call, I was lost in an endless stream of texts. Gradually, I retreated from my social life. Under the pretense of studying, I spent entire evenings hidden beneath my comforter, whispering into the phone as though it were my lifeline.

One night, I was still hunched over my notes at the dining-room table long after midnight when Yazid, who typically rose at dawn for morning prayers, called to see why I was up so late. We were deep in conversation when my father quietly entered the room. Upon seeing me on the phone, he paused, his face etched with concern, sighed, and slipped away without a word.

The next morning, bleary-eyed over breakfast, he finally spoke without preamble:

"Sweetheart, I know you miss each other, and the phone feels like your only connection. But distance makes you idealize the other person. Your mind fills in whatever you don't know with what you wish to be true," he said gravely.
"With those calls, you capture only fragments. No matter how much you talk, you'll never see the whole person."

He offered no chance for rebuttal; he simply walked out of the kitchen, leaving me to reflect. His words stung, and a part of me agreed: through a screen, you can never grasp every facet of someone's character.

His caution echoed in my head for days. I found myself observing couples around me, how they shared routines, traditions, even cultural references. Yazid and I, by contrast, seemed to share little beyond our calls. Yet perhaps our differences held their own richness, a depth that homogeneity could never provide. I reminded myself that, even at a distance, our conversations felt raw and meaningful, maybe more so than everyday chatter among those who lived side by side.

Still, I knew this situation couldn't last forever. My father's doubts would only fade once we found a concrete path forward, and forging that path would not be easy. I couldn't uproot my entire future for him, nor could he abandon his life to come to Spain.

Finally, one afternoon, during one of our calls, I voiced the question that had been haunting me: "Yazid, we have to do something if we want this to work. This distance is wearing me down. I feel as if we're stuck, going nowhere."

He hesitated, then spoke softly: "I know… Being glued to our phones isn't healthy. You already know what I think."

I pressed for clarity: "What do you mean?"

"I mean I think you should come with me to the U.S.," he said. "You worry about your English or that you don't know the country, or that it's so far from Spain, but think about it: we could both grow professionally there, and we'd finally be together. Your English is excellent, aren't we communicating in it already?"

In that moment, he laid out a plan, one I had not dared to imagine.

"You're right, but I need to think about it. The thought of a life so far away, in the U.S., scares me, even though I can't think of any other solution that would be fair for both of us."

That conversation planted a seed that slowly began to grow in my mind. If we truly wanted to be together, to share our days and our lives, we needed a plan. The distance couldn't go on forever, and if we didn't put an end to it, it would eventually put an end to us. Maybe the United States wasn't such a bad idea after all. Yazid was planning to do his residency there, and I could do the same. To me, the U.S. felt like a distant, cold place, but I knew that if I was with Yazid, I'd be okay, location wouldn't matter.

Besides, it was a country built by immigrants, and its diversity of races and cultures meant anyone could find their place. After several conversations with Yazid and a lot of internal dialogue, I decided to give it a try, to pursue that shared future we both longed for. Maybe that country could be the perfect place for us to become doctors without having to give up being together.

I started researching the process. Yazid had mentioned it before: the three exams, the study materials, the application system, but I'd never paid much attention. I never thought it would actually matter to me. For days, I read through online forums for international students, taking notes on the steps involved. Those forums were full of advice and guides for successfully becoming a medical resident in the U.S., a long and very different process compared to Spain, where a single exam determines your fate. In the U.S., beyond the exams, you also needed a personal statement explaining why you wanted to do your residency, letters of recommendation from doctors you'd impressed during your clinical rotations, research experience… I filled several pages of my notebook with notes. It all felt overwhelming at first, but I broke it down into smaller steps and promised myself I'd fight for it.

I figured one of the best first steps would be to do a clinical rotation in the U.S. That way, I could get a sense of the country and its healthcare system, and it would help me decide whether to pursue training there. With a bit of luck, I might even earn a letter of recommendation and learn more about the exams.

I didn't have any contacts in the U.S. and had no idea how to arrange a rotation, but I decided to approach several doctors at my university. Surely someone would have a connection I could use to arrange a summer placement.

I met with several physicians, first in Cardiology, then Pulmonology, but had no luck until I walked into the office of the head of the Neurology Department. Thankfully, Neurology had been one of my favorite subjects, and I'd done well on the exam, so he held me in high regard. Maybe it was luck, or maybe coincidence, but it turned out he had lived and worked in the U.S., and one of his close friends from medical school, a fellow Spaniard, was now working in Cleveland. It wasn't the most famous city in the U.S., but it would be a great place to start.

Cleveland marked the beginning of my American adventure. I would spend a summer there doing clinical rotations, learning how the healthcare system worked, and improving my English. That summer would be a sacrifice, I'd miss the beach and the festivals in Asturias, and I wouldn't be able to visit Yazid. But I was betting on a long-term future with him, and I knew the effort would be worth it. From the start, Yazid supported me. Far from pressuring me to visit, he encouraged me. He knew how important this opportunity was for both of us, and that it was an investment in our future together. Besides, Yazid was also extremely busy with his father's project and was preparing for the first U.S. exam at the end of the summer, so he wouldn't have had much time either. In truth, it was good for both of us to stay focused. With a bit of luck, we could see each other when I returned from Cleveland in early September, after his exam and before classes started.

Even though Yazid supported the experience itself, he wasn't so supportive of the housing I had chosen in Cleveland. I had searched through listings on the Case Western University forums and found only two options under $500, the most I could afford. One was a room in a house owned by a medical resident, and the other belonged to an older woman who lived alone with her cat. The resident's house was a bit cheaper and closer to the hospital. It also had other roommates, which I thought would make my stay more enjoyable. It seemed like the better option, so I chose that one.

But when I told Yazid that all my housemates were male, he didn't take it well. He saw it as a provocation and completely shut down. We talked about it for hours, but I couldn't see his perspective, and he couldn't see mine. I ignored his request to choose the other house, and instead of taking his concerns seriously, I stood my ground and refused to change my decision. What I didn't realize at the time, what I didn't even consider important, was that this conflict would mark the beginning of the end.

11

June 27, 2014

Cleveland, Ohio, United States

After a layover at the New York airport, I landed in Cleveland. It was six o'clock in the evening local time, but one in the morning back in Spain. I was exhausted. As I watched other travelers' luggage go by, waiting for mine, I couldn't help thinking about the consequences this trip might bring. I desperately hoped it would be a positive experience and that I would end up liking this country. Living in the United States was the only way I could imagine a future with Yazid.

That summer in Cleveland was going to be very different from the previous one. This time, there would be no group of students I could relate to and spend my free time with. There would be no one like Mohammed to guide me or answer my questions during those first few days. Fortunately, I wasn't entirely alone. Tom, the resident I had rented a room from, had offered to pick me up at the airport. A few days before my flight, we had a video call where he explained some basic things about the city, the house I'd be living in, and the people I'd be sharing it with.

Tom was waiting in the arrivals area, parked in his old red station wagon. He recognized me quickly, got out of the car, and came over to greet me and help with my luggage. He was tall and thin, wearing a loose-fitting gray shirt and black pants. His hospital ID badge was still hanging from his neck.

"Hi, Lola! Welcome to Cleveland," he said with a smile. He had a big mouth with perfectly aligned teeth. His eyes, on the other hand, were small and squinted when he smiled.

"Hi, Tom! Thank you so much for picking me up. You have no idea how much I appreciate it!" I replied as I shook his hand.

"No problem," he said, brushing it off. "I just got out of the clinic, which is right nearby, so it worked out perfectly. Plus, it's Friday!"

"Thank you, really," I repeated with another smile.

Tom grabbed my suitcase and, with some effort, placed it in the trunk. Then he walked over to the passenger door and opened it for me, inviting me to get in. I wasn't used to gestures like that, and I was pleasantly surprised to see that guys in the U.S., like in Jordan, still did things like that. I got in and looked around the inside of the car. It was pretty worn out and not very clean. The black leather steering wheel was faded and cracked from the sun. The cabin itself was poorly maintained, with stains on both the ceiling and the seats. There were empty bottles and crumpled papers scattered across the floor. Coffee-stained mugs filled all four cup holders between our seats. The only neat thing in the entire car was his white coat, freshly pressed and hanging from the headrest of his seat. He apologized for the mess and started the car.

The airport was about half an hour from the city, and during that time, I got to learn a bit more about Tom. He was a second-year family medicine resident at the Cleveland Clinic, one of the most prestigious hospitals in the country. His family lived in Toledo, a city about two hours west. Although he had lived in Ohio all his life, he was passionate about traveling, loved discovering other cultures, and took off on the first flight he could whenever the opportunity arose.

As we neared the neighborhood, Tom took a detour to show me the medical campus where the hospitals were located. One of them was University Hospitals, where I'd be doing my internship, and the other was the Cleveland Clinic, world-renowned. It wasn't uncommon for millionaires from around the globe to fly in on their private jets to be treated there. According to Tom, the two hospitals had a fierce rivalry. Still, they collaborated on research projects and sometimes even shared patients.

I was surprised by how beautiful the area was. It was obvious that a lot of money had been invested there. The gardens were immaculately maintained, and the sidewalks looked spotless. We left the campus behind and drove up Fairmount Avenue, where leafy trees shaded the street. We entered Cleveland Heights, one of the most exclusive neighborhoods in the city, filled with mansions. They were the most beautiful and spectacular houses I had ever seen. I was surprised that there weren't any walls or fences separating their yards from the street. Anyone could walk right up to the front door, unthinkable in Spain.

At an intersection, Tom turned onto a side street called Scarborough and left those dreamlike mansions behind. Although there were still single-family homes and trees lining the sidewalks, the houses were much more modest. The streets reminded me of suburban neighborhoods in American movies or The Simpsons' neighborhood. All the houses were painted in pastel colors and had those signature front lawns with perfect grass. It was peaceful, and barely any cars passed by. I pictured kids playing ball on Sunday afternoons.

The car slowed down, it looked like we had arrived.

Tom parked in front of a purple house. Ours house. He grabbed my luggage and motioned for me to follow him. It was very hot. To my surprise, instead of heading for the front door, he turned and walked around to the back. Just before going in, he suddenly stopped. With a gesture, he indicated that I should go ahead and open the door, it didn't need a key. That was another thing that caught my attention. Apparently, in that neighborhood, it was common practice to leave the door unlocked. I hesitantly pushed it open and stepped inside.

There was a small entryway filled with bicycles, and I could hear murmurs. It smelled like onions and garlic, a scent that transported me back home for a few seconds. Tom leaned my suitcase against a wall, and when he saw I was standing there frozen, he took the lead:

"Guys! Lola just got here!" he called out, peeking into the living room, which was an open space connected to the kitchen. He motioned for me to follow him.

"Hey! Welcome!" several voices called out almost in unison. They sounded genuinely happy that I had arrived.

"Hi!" I replied loudly, though a bit shyly, as I followed Tom and peeked into the kitchen. It looked like everyone was there.

There was a relaxed atmosphere in the house, with jazz music playing in the background and dinner being prepared. They all introduced themselves with a smile and a handshake. I made a special effort to remember their names, repeating them several times in my head.

Without spending much time chatting, Tom guided me to my room. The house had creaky wooden floors and three stories. My room was on the second floor, in one of the corners, with two windows that let in the soft light of sunset. It wasn't very big, but it had everything I needed: a bed, a desk, and a wardrobe. He showed me where the bathroom was and handed me a couple of towels. He postponed the rest of the house tour for another time and went back downstairs to join the others. He gave me some privacy to settle in and take a shower.

The door didn't have a lock, which made me feel a bit uneasy, after all, I was in a house full of strangers. I tried not to dwell on it too much. If I got paranoid at night, I figured I could always block the door with my suitcase. I took a quick shower and went down to the kitchen.

They were cooking risotto, unhurriedly, with wine and weed. I joined the conversation, and little by little, I started learning about my new housemates. Chris, a recent engineering graduate, was tall and thin like Tom and loved rock climbing. He was planning to move to Barcelona and kept asking me questions about Spain, eager for advice. Sam was the oldest of the group, but he had a childlike spirit and a small frame. He worked as a musician and a waiter at a prestigious restaurant in Cleveland, and he loved to cook. Then there was Michael, who had similar interests to Sam, he was also a musician and taught cooking classes to kids at one of the city's alternative schools. Lastly, there was Calvin, who was from Paris and doing research at the Cleveland Clinic. He was very friendly and had a strong French accent.

They all seemed genuinely happy to have me there. I felt lucky to have landed in a house like that. The risotto was delicious, I had two servings. I was so comfortable I could've stayed up talking with them all night, but between the travel and the jet lag, I desperately needed sleep.

Before closing my eyes, I sent a message to Yazid to let him know I had arrived safely and everything was fine. Since it was seven hours earlier in Amman, he was already awake and called me. He still hadn't come to terms with the fact that I had chosen that house to stay in, and once again asked me to find somewhere else, someplace where my housemates wouldn't be all men. He just couldn't see things from my perspective. He felt I had disrespected him. He kept insisting I had done it on purpose to test him.

I, on the other hand, saw things completely differently and couldn't understand his reaction. It hurt that instead of focusing on the fact that I was there for us, to fight for our future together, all he cared about was that I was living with four guys. Maybe I was being selfish or a bit naïve, but to me, that house was perfect. My housemates could show me around the city, I could have fun outside of the hospital, improve my English... I trusted myself, and I was in love with Yazid in a way I had never loved anyone before. I was doing all of this for him, for us. What more proof did he need?

That night, I didn't feel like arguing, so I ended the conversation by telling him his demand was irrational and that I was staying right where I was. Yazid got upset and ended the call with a curt, "We'll talk later. I have to go," a phrase loaded with unspoken words and feelings.

I guess sometimes intentions just aren't enough to justify our actions in the eyes of someone else, especially when that person sees the world through a completely different lens.

12

That conversation with Yazid really affected me, not just because of how vulnerable I felt being far from home, but also because his reaction struck me as unfair. Our perspectives, or realities, were so different. No matter how much I tried to put myself in his shoes, I couldn't understand his point of view. What I didn't realize then was that his reaction came from a fear of losing me, from the possibility that what had happened with Daniel the previous summer might happen with him too. But to me, that fear seemed irrational. The only reason I was there was for us to be together. I thought I had already proven how much I loved him, how deeply in love I was. The more I thought about it, the more absurd it all seemed.

The only way to solve it was either for him to come around or for me to change accommodations, but I never even considered that second option. I decided to give him some space to think. I was convinced I was right and that, sooner or later, he would see it too. But what I didn't understand at the time was that things looked very different from Yazid's point of view. After all, we both had a piece of the truth, and everything depended on how you looked at it.

Even though I couldn't stop thinking about Yazid for a second and felt saddened by the situation, that weekend I tried to clear my mind and enjoy Cleveland as much as I could. My housemates were really friendly and had made me feel welcome from the start. Sam had been given a few tickets for a Cleveland Indians baseball game, the city's team, and invited Calvin and me to join him.

I had never seen a baseball game and was curious. I was expecting a completely different atmosphere, a packed stadium full of tense fans glued to the game—but what I found was something else entirely. The pace was rather slow, and it didn't seem like a big deal to miss a play if you were late or needed to go to the restroom. Lots of people showed up after the game had already started or left early to avoid traffic. For most spectators, the game was secondary. It felt more like an excuse to hang out, drink beer, and eat hot dogs or nachos with cheese. The crowd wasn't nearly as loud as at a soccer match in Spain. The only real moments of focus came when the entire stadium coordinated to raise their arms and do the wave. There was also a sense of anticipation whenever the kiss cam turned on, recording spectators during the breaks. If your image appeared on the stadium's giant screens, you had to kiss your partner. So many movie clichés played out that afternoon, it felt like I was an extra in a Hollywood film.

The rest of the weekend I spent at home getting ready for the internship, which would begin Monday. Calvin took me grocery shopping at the local supermarket, and Chris helped me get the bike Tom had lent me in shape so I could ride it to the hospital. That house always seemed to have music playing, whether from the radio or live. Michael and Sam often practiced in the living room. They frequently invited other musician friends over to play or just hang out. In fact, that Sunday they hosted a barbecue in the backyard. While some grilled burgers and sausages, others strummed guitars and played songs. Michael was incredibly talented, he seemed to master every instrument he touched: guitar, piano, harmonica.

After that calm and easy-going weekend, everything changed drastically on Monday. It was barely six-thirty in the morning when I set out for the hospital, pedaling my bike through the first rays of sunlight. I had memorized the route the night before and was mentally retracing the map as I crossed the streets.

When I arrived at the hospital, I breathed a sigh of relief, I hadn't gotten lost. I parked my bike in a small rack by the entrance and tucked my shirt into my pants. I walked nervously toward the imposing building, excited to discover what this place and this experience would be like. I hoped I would enjoy it, and at the same time, I felt the pressure to do well. My first letter of recommendation would depend on how I performed during that rotation. That letter was one of the key components for applying to a residency at a hospital.

I stepped into the main lobby. It was massive, with high ceilings, and it reminded me more of a hotel entrance. As I looked around for the elevator, doctors and residents passed me by with hurried steps and automatic gestures, paying me no attention. I went up to the third floor, where the Neurosciences unit was located, the inpatient area for patients with neurological conditions. Elsewhere in the hospital was a tower called the Neurological Institute, which housed outpatient clinics and the subspecialties of neurology: epilepsy, dementia, multiple sclerosis, and stroke among the most prominent. I was impressed by the level of specialization. Doing a residency in a place like that was an incredible opportunity.

I was supposed to meet Dr. Ramos in the residents' workroom. After wandering around and getting lost on the floor, I decided to ask the nurses. They seemed busy, and without even pausing, one of them pointed to the room with a nod and went back to her work.

Embarrassed, I stepped inside. The room was small, with hardly any space between a couch, a square table with chairs, and the computer area, where two residents were sitting. I immediately sensed their surprise. It seemed like no one was expecting me, no one had told them it was my first day.

"Hi, what's your name? Are you one of the med students?" said one of them in a low voice. "I'm Marc, a second-year resident." After introducing himself, he turned back to his computer screen and resumed typing at full speed.

"Hi, nice to meet you." I tried to soften my accent and speak slowly, I knew that was one of my weak points. "I'm here to rotate with Dr. Ramos."

"Oh, hi!" said a petite blonde woman. "I'm Ashley, a fourth-year resident. Nice to meet you. Dr. Ramos didn't tell us anything. Do you have your ID or login credentials for the computer?"

"No, I just got here, actually." I was confused and hadn't realized I would need a badge. "Where is Dr. Ramos?"

"He won't be here until nine. Don't worry, this always happens," said Ashley in the same neutral tone. "You can go see Doris Jackson, she handles that stuff. Go to the South Building, fourth floor, office fifty-six. She'll help you with the process." Ashley jotted the number on a piece of paper and smiled as she handed it to me. "If we weren't so busy, I'd walk you over. Sorry." She turned back to her computer and started typing too.

This wasn't the kind of welcome I had imagined. A wave of insecurity swept over me, and I started to feel like I didn't belong there. The residents had assumed I knew what I was supposed to do, but Dr. Ramos hadn't explained anything. Because of my lack of experience, and perhaps my naivety, I had thought I just needed to show up. Confused, I grabbed my backpack, folded up my white coat from the University of Oviedo, and went off to find this Doris Jackson.

I spent the entire morning going from office to office: first the ID badge, then confidentiality forms. All the paperwork felt a bit absurd. At last, with everything completed, I returned to the

109

resident workroom. It was eleven-thirty, and the residents had just finished rounding and were discussing the patients' tests and treatments. Dr. Ramos was there now, sitting at the head of the table. He had a prominent forehead with deep receding hairlines, gray hair, and round glasses. He wore a purple bow tie that clashed completely with his blue shirt. He looked up and, upon seeing me, his expression changed.

"Hi, Lola! I'm Dr. Ramos. Nice to meet you. Sorry I didn't warn you about the admin stuff. Honestly, I just forgot," he said in Spanish, smiling warmly. He seemed like a good person. "If you'd like, we could grab some lunch and chat a bit."

"Sure, that sounds great," I replied shyly. Given his initial indifference, I hadn't expected him to invite me to lunch.

"Give me ten minutes," he said, switching to English as he wrapped up the patient list with the team.

We went to the cafeteria, which had high, translucent ceilings that let in natural light. There were plants in every corner and even between the tables. It was a pleasant space. The cafeteria offered a wide range of food: from pizza to sushi, plus salads you could build yourself with custom ingredients. Despite all the options, I couldn't find the classic Spanish tortilla or a ham and cheese sandwich. Dr. Ramos went for pizza, and out of courtesy, I did the same, even though I really felt like having a salad. We sat at one of the tables.

Despite his busy schedule, we talked for almost two hours, until he was interrupted by a call for an emergency he had to attend to. Dr. Ramos told me about his background, life in the U.S., and his family. He had completed his residency in Spain but later moved to Boston to pursue research. That was nearly fifteen years ago. He did his neurology residency at Harvard and specialized in stroke. To my surprise, he didn't miss Spain at all and was quite happy living in the U.S., especially because of his salary, which allowed him to travel wherever he wanted, whenever his schedule permitted. He worked too much and only got about two weeks of vacation per year.

He had met his wife three years earlier in Cleveland. She was Taiwanese, and they had welcomed a baby girl the previous year. Dr. Ramos had successfully built a life in the U.S. and had no intention of returning to Spain.

That introductory Monday was the shortest day of the week. After lunch with Ramos, I headed home. The rest of the days, though, I spent more than ten hours at the hospital. I wasn't used to such long days or waking up so early, it was a real struggle. On top of that, speaking English took extra mental effort. I came home exhausted and completely drained.

I also had to go in on Saturdays, which in Spain would have been unthinkable. Things were very different here, and much more was expected of students. At the hospital in Oviedo, we usually took a passive role, just observing while the doctor or resident talked to the patient. But here, students were expected to speak with patients and examine them themselves.

The structure of work was also different. Before rounding with the attending, the students and residents would first visit the patients and prepare a plan. That way, when the doctor arrived, Dr. Ramos in this case, all the patients had already been seen and evaluated.

I was rotating with two medical students who were way ahead of me. They were much more confident with the patients and conducted the neurological exam quickly and systematically, as if it came effortlessly. Unlike them, I often forgot parts of the physical exam, whether checking reflexes or coordination. I'd realize it afterward and would have to go back to the room to finish.

Also, even though many of the patients had difficulty articulating due to their neurological conditions, I often struggled to understand their accents, which I found thick. The same thing happened with the residents—not only when they talked about casual topics, but even when they discussed patient cases and diagnoses. They used abbreviations I had never heard before, and I felt embarrassed to ask. So I'd quietly write the words down in my notebook and look them up later online.

In general, the residents were friendly and did their best to help me whenever they could. Little by little, I got to know their stories and found that many of them, like me, were foreigners. For the most part, they were quite serious and tended to keep work and personal life separate. Once their shifts were over, everyone went home. Maybe they were just busy or tired, but in Spain, residents usually made plans together and developed a different kind of bond, more familiar, more personal. I loved sharing a house with the guys, making weekend plans, or simply having someone to talk to when I got home. If I had chosen to live with that older lady, I would have felt much more alone.

As the days went by, I quietly missed Yazid and couldn't stop thinking about him. It was agonizing not to write, but I had

112

decided it had to be him who made the first move. Nearly two weeks passed before we finally resumed contact. His message was neutral, he said he wanted to talk over video call. I couldn't quite grasp his intentions, and I was struck by how cold his words felt. Even so, and despite still feeling hurt, I was glad he had reached out. I tried to get a hint of what he wanted to talk about, but he just said, "I'll tell you when we talk."

I woke up on Sunday thinking about our upcoming conversation. I wondered whether he had something specific to say or just wanted to make peace. After such a cryptic message, I didn't know what to expect. The night before, we'd had a barbecue in the backyard, and I'd drunk too much beer, my head was pounding. As usual, the guys had invited friends over and spent the evening playing music and drinking. Luckily, I wasn't always the only girl at those gatherings, several of their girlfriends and our next-door neighbor, Lisa, had joined us the night before.

I messaged Yazid. I was hungry, and since he was taking a while to reply, I went downstairs to grab a slice of bread with Nutella, my go-to breakfast in Cleveland. As I walked down the stairs, I followed the smell of butter and the sound of voices coming from the kitchen. Calvin was making pancakes with Sam.

"Good morning! What a hangover," Calvin greeted me as he saw me reaching for the Nutella jar. "Want to have breakfast with us?"

"Good morning, guys. I'd love to, but I need to make a call first, it shouldn't take more than half an hour," I replied, trying to downplay the conversation I was about to have, though my stomach was already tight with nerves.. "Will you let me know

113

when everything's ready?"

"Sure thing," Sam smiled. "We'll make some for you too."

I headed back upstairs with a glass of water, set my laptop on the bed, and sat on the wooden floor. Yazid had messaged saying he was already on Skype. I logged in too, a knot tightening in my stomach.

I was happy to see him, even if only on a screen. He looked serious, with a hint of sadness. We made small talk, about everything and nothing. It felt like he wanted to say something but couldn't decide whether to go through with it. He asked me about Cleveland and the hospital. He told me he had his first American board exam coming up in just a couple of weeks, about a month earlier than originally planned.

After circling around it, he finally opened up.

"Lola, you know when you hide a box of chocolates in your room because you're afraid someone will eat them when you're not there?" He looked away. "That's how I feel about you. Having you so far away gives me anxiety and fear. I can't trust you if you stay in that house."

"I don't understand why you feel that way, Yazid. You know why I'm here. They treat me well, they're kind and respectful. I'm asking you, please, to trust me…"

"And I'm asking you, please, to move out. I can't keep going like this. I'm sorry." He lowered his gaze.

That whole conversation still felt unfair to me, his reaction was disproportionate and selfish. As I tried to explain and we kept going in circles, Sam knocked on my door.

"Hey! The pancakes are ready," he called, and his footsteps faded down the hall.

Yazid's expression twisted with frustration, and he abruptly ended the call. It seemed like that was the excuse he needed to bring things to an end.

"It's obvious you're doing just fine there. I see where your priorities lie, Lola. You don't care about my feelings, and I can't live like this." He paused, struggling to say the words. "I think it's best if we forget about each other. I have to go. Goodbye."

He disconnected before I could say a word. The room went silent, and a deep sadness came over me. I cried. I shut the laptop, and my reflection on the dark screen looked back at me, absurd and empty. Was I really doing something so wrong? I couldn't believe our relationship was ending like this, after everything I was sacrificing for us.

13

That conversation marked the end of our relationship. His reaction had been disproportionate and unfair, he'd projected his insecurities onto my actions. I realized then that the only way to fix things between us would be for me to move out of that house. But I knew that giving in to such an irrational demand would only be the first of many sacrifices. As painful as it was, staying true to myself had to come first. I wasn't going to give in.

Even though I was convinced I was right, the days that followed were difficult. Now that we were no longer together, staying in that house felt pointless. Suddenly, my time in Cleveland had lost its meaning, and without Yazid in my life, I struggled to find the motivation to keep going. It took me several days to shift my mindset and begin to enjoy and appreciate the experience again.

As the weeks passed, things at the hospital improved. I gradually began to understand more of what the residents and patients were saying. The abbreviations that had once sounded like gibberish began to repeat themselves, and now that I knew what they meant, everything started to click. I had mastered the neurological exam and even managed to surprise Dr. Ramos by presenting patients with the confidence of a local student.

Every morning, I was the first to leave the house. Sometimes I'd run into Chris, who woke up as early as I did, and he'd offer to drive me if it was raining. Other times, if the rain started in the afternoon, Sam would swing by the hospital to pick me up. Both of them had cars with huge trunks, so transporting my bike was never an issue. They all looked after me like I was their little sister.

In the evenings, we each tended to eat dinner at different times. When a few of us happened to be around at the same time, we'd gather around the large dining table or sit outside in the garden, talking about our problems or just life in general.

One night, several days after that last conversation with Yazid, we had one of our "family dinners," as Michael liked to call them. Afterward, we headed out to the backyard and sat in lawn chairs around the fire pit. We'd been drinking wine, and the atmosphere was mellow. Lisa, our neighbor, had brought weed from Colorado. As we passed the joint around, the conversation turned to romantic relationships.

Calvin talked about his bad luck with love, both in France and in the U.S. He still hadn't met anyone he genuinely connected with. He had profiles on several dating apps, but all he ever found were superficial encounters. With so many options, he said, it always felt like there might be someone better just a swipe away.

That constant sense of endless possibilities made him lose interest quickly.

I found his perspective fascinating, I knew nothing about online dating. Back in Spain, none of my friends or acquaintances used those apps. Maybe the U.S. was ahead of us when it came to trends in love. I, however, preferred something more traditional, more genuine. As the joint came my way, Calvin gave me a look and motioned for me to share my thoughts.

No long explanation was necessary. Everyone there, in one way or another, already knew about Yazid, I'd mentioned him when explaining why I was in Cleveland. Lisa knew the full story; she had become my support system in the city and was aware of my recent conversation with him. The others only knew the basics and assumed our relationship was still intact.

When I told them we'd broken up because he wanted me to move out and didn't trust me, or them, their expressions changed. There was a brief silence, and then Michael said something that really made me think:

"His reaction is unfair, Lola. But you have to understand, he's not here to see who we really are or how you act around us. Sometimes our minds play tricks on us, and our thoughts distort how we perceive reality."

Michael was about three years older than me. He was empathetic and thoughtful, he reminded me of Daniel, with his open and understanding outlook on life. His words gave me much-needed perspective, and that night, I began to see things a little more from Yazid's point of view.

I started to grasp how much he must have been struggling with the situation, and the resentment I had been carrying began to ease. I knew that my past, cheating on Daniel, had planted seeds of insecurity in Yazid. Combined with the distance between us and my choice to live in a house full of men, it was no surprise that his fear had grown. In the end, Yazid had no way to be sure of how I was behaving.

I thought about writing to him and trying to make things right, but I knew that unless I moved out of the house, he wouldn't budge. I missed him, but I chose silence, I needed time to think.

Summer continued in Cleveland, and July gave way to August. Dr. Ramos and the neurology residents completed their rotation, and Dr. Johnson took over. His style was completely different. He was one of the department's oldest and most respected doctors, and a favorite among the residents.

Short and bald, he had a perfectly shaved, shiny head that practically invited you to touch it. Like Dr. Ramos, he wore a bow tie and always buttoned his white coat all the way to the top. He loved joking around with everyone, even the patients, but still managed to maintain professionalism and respect.

It wasn't that Dr. Ramos was any less competent or kind, but he was definitely more serious, and the residents didn't seem as relaxed around him. Maybe being younger, foreign, and having an accent made Dr. Ramos feel like he had to be stricter to earn their respect.

The medical students changed in August, too. Among the new arrivals was Rahim, from Pakistan. He was very friendly, and

120

we quickly hit it off. He told me that medicine, and life in general, in his country weren't going very well, and that he wanted to pursue a neurology residency in the United States. He was planning to apply that fall, in the next cycle. He reminded me of the Jordanian students I'd met before. I began to better understand why so many international medical students came from countries dealing with conflict or unstable economies. In the end, they were all searching for stability.

Rahim was doing that rotation to get the last letter of recommendation he needed, and he was hoping to secure an interview at that hospital. His older brother was an internal medicine resident in Detroit and had helped guide him through the process.

I told him a bit of my own story, without mentioning Yazid, and shared that, like him, I was also considering doing my residency in the U.S. Talking to Rahim made me feel understood and helped me grasp more of how the American system worked. He offered to lend me his notes and explained in great detail which books I should read to score well on the exams.

Now that Yazid and I were no longer together, the idea of doing a residency in the U.S. was up in the air, but I had to admit I was beginning to consider it as something independent of our relationship. Over those weeks, I had come to see that the training residents received there was outstanding, and that it would be a transformative experience academically, personally, and in life in general. I really appreciated the cultural diversity among the residents, people from Taiwan, Colombia, Egypt, and beyond, and how much emphasis they placed on scientific rigor.

They stayed up to date with the latest published research and used it to guide many of their treatment decisions.

I loved that every day at lunchtime there was a lecture on a topic or disease. During that hour, the residents would pause their clinical duties to eat together and learn something new. Doing a residency in the U.S. would undoubtedly be harder than in Spain, but I could always return, and my experience would be highly valued. For all these reasons, the idea, one I never would've considered had it not been for Yazid, was gaining more and more strength.

After talking with Rahim and hearing the perspectives of other international residents, I decided that training as a doctor in the U.S. would be an incredible opportunity. I was going to fight for it, and I was doing it for me. Whether or not Yazid was in my life wouldn't change that. Deep down, though, I still held onto the hope that things between us might eventually work out, and that we could still pursue our dream of being together in the U.S.

Rahim, who was an expert on the process, gave me tons of advice. One of his suggestions was to get involved in research while preparing for the American exams. He explained that every year, thousands of international students applied for residency positions, and the competition kept increasing. In addition to good test scores, you needed something else to stand out. Having research experience and published articles in scientific journals could make a huge difference.

The days went by, moving between the hospital and home, and suddenly September arrived. Summer had slipped by almost without me noticing. On the last day of my rotation, I said goodbye to my colleagues, and to Dr. Ramos as well. They all supported my decision to pursue residency in the U.S. and offered to help me with anything I might need. I felt incredibly supported.

On my way home, I thought about how much I had grown, both personally and professionally, over those three months. I had completed my first neurology rotation in the U.S., and aside from learning so much about the field, the experience had helped me decide on my future: to apply for residency in that country. On top of that, I had earned my first letter of recommendation, a key part of the application process.

On a personal level, I'd learned more about myself, met people from different cultures, many of whom had become friends, and gained a broader understanding of the world. I had managed to get by on a tight budget, and most importantly, I had learned to rely on myself.

The only truly painful part of that summer had been the breakup with Yazid. I still struggled to process it, but I knew that, at least for now, there was no resolution.

I returned to Spain on September 5th, excited to see my family and friends, and the sea. I was going to miss Cleveland, and my days on Scarborough street, living in the purple house.

14

I arrived on a Saturday morning at Asturias Airport. The scent of the sea and my father's embrace were the first to greet me. I was so happy to be home. I had missed life in Gijón and was eager to savor the last days of summer. In a week, Sara and I would be celebrating our birthdays, and my parents were planning a family barbecue to mark the occasion. Those gatherings were my favorite. I loved the idea of sitting around a table piled high with food, surrounded by uncles, aunts, and cousins. I was also really looking forward to seeing my friends again.

Though I was thrilled to be back in Gijón, I couldn't stop thinking about Yazid and how things had ended between us, it made me deeply sad. It had been over a month since we last spoke, and the silence between us hurt more than I'd expected. I kept wondering how he was feeling, whether he still missed me or thought about us. I fought the urge to reach out to him constantly. My friends asked about him, and when I told them we had broken up, they were surprised. I avoided giving them details and felt embarrassed to explain the real reason for our breakup. They wouldn't have understood, just as I hadn't at first, and the moment I told them what had happened, all those stereotypes about the Arab world would have come flooding in. I brushed it off and quickly changed the subject, masking how much his silence hurt and how deeply I still missed him.

On the morning of my birthday, I woke up smiling, eager to celebrate with my family. I stretched under the covers as the soft hum of my parents and sister talking in the kitchen floated up, they were discussing the lunch preparations. I was still recovering from jet lag and adjusting to Spanish time, so I was the last one to get up. I felt tired and didn't want to leave the warmth of my bed, but there was much to do, and I knew my parents would appreciate the help. Before heading downstairs, I grabbed my phone from the nightstand and hid under the covers. I turned off airplane mode and logged into Facebook to check my notifications and birthday wishes. There were messages from college friends and high school classmates... then a message from Yazid popped up.

I was genuinely happy that he'd remembered my birthday, and even more so that he'd reached out, despite how things had ended.

"Happy birthday! I hope you're doing well and enjoying your day."

It was short and neutral. I was dying to reply, and unlike the other messages, which I left for later, I responded to his immediately. He was online, and we started chatting. At first, our tone was distant; neither of us knew quite how to act. But little by little, the conversation loosened up and our emotions resurfaced. There were still so many feelings between us, and it was clear Yazid wanted to revisit what had happened in Cleveland. We picked up right where we'd left off. I couldn't quite read the tone of his messages or figure out what he was trying to say. It felt as though my birthday was just an excuse to talk again, only to reproach me once more for my lack of empathy.

It didn't feel like the right time to rehash everything, and I was exhausted by the fact that we weren't making any progress. We ended the conversation on bad terms, and I realized that talking wouldn't fix things, especially not at a distance. All the joy I'd felt that morning vanished. We still didn't understand each other. I resigned myself to the idea that we were truly over. After that chat, we never spoke again, though deep down I still hoped things might change one day.

The weeks, and even months, that followed were dreary. As time went on, I missed Yazid more and more, and the silence only intensified those feelings. That longing became a vicious cycle, eventually spiraling into a quiet depression I kept hidden behind my bedroom walls. I didn't want to see anyone and hid away under the guise of studying. I avoided my friends and had no interest in spending time with my parents or my sister, who grew worried about my changed behavior.

One afternoon, toward the end of lunch as we sat around the table, my mom—tired of seeing me like that, gently suggested a change: "Sweetheart, why don't you join a gym and get some exercise?" she asked, concern in her voice. "You spend way too much time studying." She popped a piece of pineapple into her mouth. "One of my coworkers told me they opened a new gym near the football stadium. It even has a pool and a spa."

"Thanks, Mom. That actually sounds like a great idea," I said, taking a sip of coffee and letting the suggestion sink in.

I hadn't considered it before, but joining a gym seemed perfect. It might break the mental rut I was stuck in, and maybe even help me meet new people. A week later, I signed up.

The facility was modern and had everything imaginable: tons of group classes, a huge room filled with cardio machines and free weights to suit any routine, and of course, the pool and spa my mom had mentioned.

One Saturday in December, on one of those dark afternoons after a full day of studying, I decided to head to the spa. I found great comfort in running along the beach and ending the day unwinding in the jacuzzi.

It was eight o'clock in the evening, and the gym would close in an hour. Hardly anyone was left, and with the darkness outside, the place had taken on a quiet, intimate atmosphere. I slipped into a bikini from last summer, wrapped myself in a towel, and headed to the spa. I opened the door to the heated section and, as I draped my towel over a chair, a familiar voice called my name.

"Lola!"

Daniel was leaning against the edge of the pool. "What are you doing here?"

I froze in surprise, definitely not expecting to run into anyone I knew, least of all him. He climbed out of the water and came over to greet me. His wet, curly hair fell across part of his forehead, and he still sported that signature beard. He wore short navy swim trunks; his chest was toned and his shoulders noticeably broader, it was clear he'd been working out these past few months. He looked incredibly handsome, and his warm smile and contagious optimism were exactly as I remembered.

It had been over a year since we'd last seen each other, and I'd be lying if I said I wasn't happy to see him. We caught up naturally, the conversation flowing easily as if everything that had happened between us no longer mattered. His presence brought me a sense of calm, I'd missed that energy. Carried away by the moment, I surprised myself by asking,

"Do you want to grab a drink or dinner one day next week?"

"Sure, why not!" he replied instantly. For some reason, he didn't seem surprised by my invitation.

"Great! How about next Wednesday?"

"That works perfectly," he said with a smile. "It's so good to see you! By the way, I didn't know you came to this gym. What a coincidence!"

"Yeah, I signed up about a month ago. I usually come in the afternoons, never this late, but…" I returned his smile.

"I usually come in the mornings, but I couldn't today. This pool is my favorite spot, especially when it's empty. Anyway, I've got to go. See you next week! Bye!"

I headed for the jacuzzi, which was empty, and sank into the warm water with my thoughts, replaying what had just happened until the gym closed. I was still in love with Yazid, but our relationship hadn't worked out and I had no choice but to move on. Now that Daniel had reappeared, I couldn't deny he was someone special to me. What I felt for him was more affection and respect than anything else, but I was still drawn to both his personality, and his physique.

We agreed to meet at nine in front of the statue of Pelayo at the marina. It was a pitch-black night, it had been raining all day, and the streets were dotted with puddles. The air was cold and damp, and the empty streets made it clear it was a weeknight. I'd been studying all day and my mind felt overloaded, yet I was eager to see him.

I arrived five minutes late and found Daniel leaning against the railing, gazing at the boats. He was wearing the same tight black jeans and low-top sneakers he always did. We hugged, and his scent immediately transported me back to our time together.

We walked along the promenade and detoured to a small sushi restaurant on a side street. It was nearly empty, aside from us, only a couple of other diners remained. As we used to, we ordered a pitcher of sake and shared several types of sushi. We had plenty to talk about: ourselves, our families, our plans.

Daniel didn't dare ask about Yazid until near the end of dinner. His expression shifted when I told him we were no longer together, that the cultural differences between us had been too great and we hadn't spoken in months. From that moment, the tone of the evening softened even more. Maybe it was the sake, but the attraction we'd tried to downplay became impossible to hide.

The restaurant was about to close, and before heading home, Daniel invited me to see the penthouse apartment he'd just moved into. It was in the city center, just a few blocks away. I knew what that invitation implied, a chance to revisit the past, and I decided to go with it.

The chemistry, the nostalgia, the shared history, it all led to that night ending in his bed. In silence, he showed me how much he'd missed me. His kisses were the soft refuge I never knew I longed for, arriving at exactly the right moment. We fell asleep in each other's arms.

The next morning, we woke up still wrapped around each other. Daniel gently stroked my back, and I savored the warmth of his fingertips. I kept my eyes closed, hovering in that liminal space between sleep and wakefulness.

"You know what?" he broke the silence.

"Tell me," I replied, moving a little closer to him.

"I've never forgotten you." He paused. "I've been waiting for this moment for a long time."

There wasn't a trace of bitterness in his voice or his feelings. Daniel didn't care about the past, focused on the present, he was ready to start over.

We talked about how things had ended between us. From his words, I could tell he had come to understand that our relationship hadn't been as full or mature as we once thought. There had been a gap between us that only widened during that summer in Amman. I admired his maturity, the clarity of his words, and his honesty, but what surprised me most was his ability to forgive.

"Lola," he said softly, placing a kiss on my shoulder, "I know that after everything that's happened, your head might still be spinning... but I'd really love for us to give our relationship a second chance. The connection I feel with you is something special, and I don't want to walk away from that."

"Baby," I whispered, kissing him back, not really sure how to respond. "I'm still so confused, but I care about you deeply, and I feel really comfortable with you… We can try and see what happens."

Yazid was still on my mind, but I chose to go with the flow.

Things took on a different hue after that night. Daniel became a light in the dark. He'd shown up just when I needed him most, bringing levity and reminding me of his world full of endless perspectives. He became my support system and helped pull me out of the hole I'd been stuck in for the past few months.

This time around, Daniel was much more present. Instead of leading separate lives, we began making more plans together. His love for me was unconditional, he showed it every chance he

132

got. He forgave me and chose to trust me again. He never once showed even the slightest hint of jealousy. He made it clear that he wanted to be with me, to spend time together, and that the past would stay where it belonged, behind us.

Daniel was the most understanding and empathetic person I had ever known. Once again, he was showing me what love truly meant.

15

The honeymoon phase with Daniel lasted for several months, during which I truly believed I had forgotten Yazid. I knew that by leaning on Daniel, I had taken the quickest path, but he understood me exactly as I was. Despite everything that had happened, he had forgiven me, and somehow, everything with him flowed smoothly, without friction.

My relationship with Yazid had made me realize how important it is to have a partner who trusts you, respects your decisions, and supports you. Daniel did all of that perfectly. He gave me freedom and walked alongside me, never pushing, never holding me back. He added to my life and never took anything away. With him, problems barely existed. Unlike Yazid, he was able to leave the past behind, allowing us to focus on the present and enjoy each other.

I often wondered how I could have treated him so badly, and at times, I regretted how I'd acted in the past. It was true that we had both grown through the process, and our relationship was now stronger: we shared much more in our day-to-day lives, and our communication was more honest. But as always, nothing was perfect, and there were still a few aspects that made me question things.

Daniel had that rare open-mindedness and the ability to forgive the unforgivable. On the one hand, it was wonderful, but on the other, it made me fear that one day the roles would reverse, and I'd be the one expected to accept something difficult.

Daniel always said that if we were together, it was because we both wanted to be, and that if our feelings ever changed, we needed to be honest with ourselves and walk away. He was incredibly sincere, he put into words what most people wouldn't dare say. But that sincerity sometimes made me fear he'd leave at the first sign of trouble.

Those fears were irrational, most likely projections of my own insecurities. After all, he had always shown me nothing but pure love, and I had been the one who betrayed his trust and ended things.

Our final year of college flew by. I spent most of it locked in my room, buried in study sessions for both my university finals and the American licensing exams. Amid that book-filled routine, I learned to appreciate the sunsets outside my window, and discovered that the most beautiful ones came on cloudy days.

Bit by bit, I began to withdraw from college life and my friends' plans. I followed their parties from a distance and sometimes wondered if I was missing something truly important, or if my efforts would pay off.

I didn't have much time for Daniel, either. He respected my study schedule and never pressured me to spend time together, so we usually met to go to the gym or study side by side. He was studying business, and his exams generally required less prep. But even when he finished early, he'd grab a book or invent something to do just to stay close during my long hours of studying.

As we neared the end of the school year, my classmates were discussing which prep courses to take for Spain's national medical residency exam, while I was becoming more and more focused on building a future in the U.S.

Those conversations reminded me how far removed I was from their path, and how different the two systems were. In Spain, everything hinged on the MIR exam. In the U.S., not only did I have to score high on three separate tests, I also needed strong letters of recommendation, application essays, and interviews. The thought of everything still ahead overwhelmed me. The fear of failure made me hide my plans from most people.

Sometimes, when I struggled to focus or had a bad day, doubts would creep in and I'd wonder whether I should even continue. I didn't trust myself enough, and fear would freeze me.

In those moments of weakness, Daniel was always there, with his calm optimism and smile. The security he gave me stood in sharp contrast to the uncertainty in our relationship and the absence of any shared plans for the future. It was a topic we never brought up. Maybe neither of us was ready, or maybe we didn't know how.

After months of avoiding it, just days after our graduation ceremony, when the uncertainty felt heavier than ever, Daniel finally brought it up. We were in his room. I was studying, and he was reading a book about design, one of his hobbies.

"Baby, I want you to know how proud I am of all the effort you're putting in to get where you want to go," he said, sitting up in bed and leaning against the wall, the open book resting on his lap. "But sometimes I wonder where our relationship is headed."

"Yeah... I feel the same," I replied, searching for what to say next. "There's still a long way to go before I'd move to the U.S., and maybe the exams won't go well, and in the end, I'll take The Spanish Residency Entrance Exam and stay in Spain."

"You're right, it's still too soon to know," he said thoughtfully, concern softening his face. "I guess it's best if we just focus on the present. No one really knows what the future holds... or what will happen between us."

His words hung in the air, and I didn't know how to keep the conversation going. That day, I realized Daniel was far more concerned about our future than I was. That conversation made me reflect, and accept that, even though this second chapter was much better than the first, we still had a long way to go.

I wasn't confident enough in our relationship to ask him to move to the United States with me. There were still several months ahead, and I hoped that in that time I'd be able to make up my mind one way or another. I couldn't understand why, after everything we'd been through and all that Daniel had shown me, I still felt so uncertain. Perhaps indecision was a decision in itself, and the best choice might be for me to go to the U.S. on my own.

Sometimes I wondered if my doubts were really about Yazid. Even though our silence had settled into a comfortable rhythm and no longer bothered me, he was always on my mind. I hated to admit it, but I still missed him.

That summer passed in a blur of textbooks, and at last I sat for my first U.S. medical board exam. I had to travel to Madrid, the only city with an accredited testing center. The seven-hour exam felt endless, and I left mentally drained. When my results arrived, my fears were confirmed: I hadn't failed, but my score was far below what I needed to be a competitive residency candidate. Still, I refused to give up.

On the online forums for international applicants, forums I had consulted so often to resolve doubts about the American process, others shared their experiences of low first-exam scores. A recurring theme was the importance of getting involved in research to stand out from the rest of the applicants and build useful connections. That idea echoed in my mind and reminded me of Rahim's advice. Reading those stories gave me the courage to try the same path: I would secure a research position to strengthen my résumé before applying for residency.

Besides advice, that forum was filled with stories of personal perseverance. It became a source of inspiration that kept me going in my pursuit of a neurology residency in the United States.

When I compared their circumstances to mine, I felt fortunate. Many were fleeing war-torn countries with limited resources, while I was pursuing this path out of intellectual curiosity and personal growth. Yes, Yazid had initially been part of the motivation, but that had since taken a backseat.

Following Rahim's advice and the forum's suggestions, I decided to write an email to various neurologist-researchers in the U.S. In it, I introduced myself and offered to help with their projects. I was fascinated by neuroimmunology, a field that explores the relationship between the immune system and the nervous system. If I could secure even a small research role in that field, I would achieve three goals at once: work in a field I loved, boost my résumé, and build professional connections.

One night, after a long day of studying and unable to focus any longer, I began searching online for the email addresses of neuroimmunology specialists. After navigating the websites of various hospitals, I identified several researchers and sent them an email, using the same message each time, only changing the greeting. I knew it was a long shot, and the odds of anyone replying or taking me seriously were slim, but I had nothing to lose. I only needed one yes, just one opportunity.

In the following days, I received nothing but rejections. Many congratulated me on my interest and wished me luck, but they either didn't have funding or didn't have any active projects. At least I had tried. I went back to the routine of my study-filled days.

Before I knew it, summer had slipped through my fingers. My birthday came and went almost without me realizing it. I hadn't looked forward to it as much as the year before, but Yazid reached out again, once more breaking the silence exactly three hundred sixty-five days later. It felt like déjà vu when he wished me a happy birthday using almost the same words.

I replied, and we started texting again, but soon we moved to a phone call that lasted two hours. Instead of blaming me for how things had ended or showing any resentment, his tone was neutral, and we spoke like old acquaintances, as if nothing had ever happened between us. His voice still had that relaxed quality, and his infectious laugh made me laugh too. He told me about his plans for the future.

"That's great, you're still fighting to train as a resident in the U.S.," he remarked, his tone more upbeat than I expected.

"Yes! I'm preparing for the second exam. The first one didn't go so well, but I'm confident I can make up for it this time," I replied, hiding my anxiety about possibly falling short of my expectations again.

"I'm sure you will! By the way, did I tell you I'm planning a trip to the U.S. in a year? We're closing some contracts in the Middle East, but if all goes well, I'll have several meetings in Chicago and along the East Coast next summer," he said enthusiastically.

"That's great. I'm not sure when I'll be there yet, maybe I'll apply for residency in the next cycle," I answered.

"Maybe we'll cross paths again, can you imagine? I wouldn't mind seeing you," he said casually.

I had completely lost track of time when my sister knocked on the door to call me down for lunch. Part of me wanted to keep talking to him, but another part felt relieved, the conversation was veering into dangerous territory, and I wasn't sure how to navigate it. I was unsettled by how, after being so hurt last year, he now acted as if nothing had happened. Sometimes I couldn't understand his behavior and found myself doubting the sincerity of his words.

Without meaning to, Yazid and I started talking more often. Still, we kept an emotional distance and never moved beyond polite conversation. It took us a couple of weeks to bring up anything personal. I didn't know why, but I couldn't bring myself to tell him I was back with Daniel, and I kept putting off the moment. When I finally told him, his reaction was… strange.

"You know, Lola? I'm not surprised. I think you two are meant for each other, and you were always his. After all, I interfered in your relationship and didn't respect it. He seems like a good guy." His voice barely shifted. His words were laced with indifference.

I hadn't expected that. It bothered me that he spoke of me as if I were someone's possession, though I reminded myself he probably meant it figuratively, as in being someone's girlfriend, not literally.

Unlike me, Yazid was still single. He'd met a few girls, but nothing serious ever developed. I was surprised at myself for feeling relieved that he hadn't found someone. I knew that if he did, especially if she was from his own culture, he likely wouldn't wait long to get married. That thought frightened me.

142

Winter came, swept in by the rhythm of study and routine. The days blurred together, and I often lost track of what day it was. They all felt the same, endless hours of studying, with only the pages in my notes changing.

One early morning, as I was finishing a chapter on diuretics, I received an email from someone I didn't recognize. It was in English. The person was offering me a research position… I couldn't recall who he was. I had long forgotten most of the emails I'd sent and had no memory of his name. I looked him up online, and my heart began to race. He was one of the top multiple sclerosis researchers in the United States. I replied immediately, and that night I couldn't sleep from excitement. My options had been slim, but now, suddenly, I had a real chance.

Everything happened fast. A week after our interview, he emailed me with a formal offer: a paid, two-year research position. I shared the news with my parents, who—though overjoyed, had mixed emotions. That same evening, I went to Daniel's place to spend the night and told him everything.

"Curly, I have to tell you something. I just got offered a research position, at Johns Hopkins! It's one of the best hospitals in the U.S. Me! I can't believe it…" I said, glowing. "I accepted. I start next May."

"Baby, I'm so happy for you!" he said, pulling me into a hug. "You've been locked away studying for months. All that effort finally paid off. This is amazing!"

"Thank you. I still can't believe I'll be moving to the U.S. in five months. Now that it's real, I'm scared, I don't know what's going to happen to me!"

"You'll be fine. You always figure out a way to make things work. This time won't be any different." He smiled, brushing a strand of hair from my face.

Daniel had always been my biggest supporter, encouraging me to chase my dreams and leave my fears behind. He believed in me more than I believed in myself, and he made me feel like I could accomplish anything.

Now that my life in the United States was about to begin, it was time to revisit that conversation about our future.

"Lola, have you thought about what's going to happen with us?" Daniel asked, his tone serious.

"I've thought about it a lot." I took a deep breath. "I'm happy with you, but I don't feel ready to ask you to leave everything behind and come with me. I'm just not that sure yet…" I looked at him, searching his face.

"I understand. It's a tough decision. I'm not even sure I'm ready to leave Gijón so soon either." He moved closer. His answer surprised me, but it comforted me to know we were feeling the same way. "You know what? Let's just go with the flow and see how it feels. I'm sure you'll come back to Gijón, and I'll be here waiting for you when you do." He kissed the tip of my nose.

Daniel kept showing how flexible he was when it came to our relationship. What he didn't know was that Yazid's shadow still lingered over me, affecting me more than I cared to admit.

16

May 18, 2016

Baltimore, Maryland, United States

The image of my father bidding me farewell at the airport as I passed through security remained etched in my mind and stayed with me throughout the trip. It marked the beginning of my new life in the United States and became the first of many goodbyes. I was filled with fear and uncertainty, and as I moved farther away from Spain, I realized that my inner child was not ready to leave Gijón.

Baltimore, a city unknown to me until just a few months earlier, would soon become my new home. For the next two years, I would be researching multiple sclerosis at Johns Hopkins Hospital. It sounded great to say, but I still had no clear idea of what my role would entail. I had thrown myself into it somewhat recklessly, dazzled by the opportunity. I had never worked in research before, and my notion of it was quite simple: I had pictured myself in a white lab coat in a lab, using pipettes and test tubes. But from the conversation I had with my future boss, I learned that my work would be very different. It would involve evaluating patients and gathering clinical data for analysis. Even after his explanations, I couldn't fully visualize it. Still, I trusted that everything would go well and that after a few months I would learn how things worked.

I was not only uncertain about what my job would be like, but I was also worried about the challenge of moving so far from home. I was used to living with my parents and having everything taken care of for me. Living alone, right upon arrival, seemed far too complicated. I wasn't prepared. I needed to acclimate to my new life, and to the city.

To ease my adjustment, I decided that in the first few months it would be easier to rent a room and have roommates who could guide me through simple tasks like setting up electricity or internet service. On the university forum, I found a guy named Aaron, who lived with his father and had a couple of rooms available. It seemed like a good option, and the house was next to the bus stop that would take me to the hospital. I contacted him and, after a quick phone call, we sealed the deal.

After a layover in Madrid and another in New York, I landed in Baltimore. I was greeted by a cold, cloudy afternoon. This time no one came to pick me up, and I had no choice but to take a taxi. I was nervous and felt insecure; I missed Gijón. Exhausted, I sank into the seat of that yellow cab and let my gaze drift over the scenery. The highway was lined with lush trees, and the late-afternoon light filtered through the branches. As we approached the city, the skyscrapers and the port on Chesapeake Bay appeared. The driver headed into downtown, taking a street that led straight to Charles Village, the neighborhood where I would live. Except for the distinctive skyline of downtown, most of the buildings were low-rise red-brick structures. Generally well kept, some looked abandoned and bore graffiti on their facades.

Baltimore was known for being like a chessboard, where from one block to the next things could change drastically. In an instant, you could go from a safe street to one where you might be robbed, even in broad daylight. Luckily, Aaron's house was on a safe street, although the ones next door were not as much.

As we went up that street, the low buildings gave way to townhouses with small front gardens. The driver slowed down and stopped at 4345 Barclay Street. We had arrived. It was a quiet residential area with little traffic; it felt safe and peaceful. I took a deep breath and exhaled, trying to release all my fear. The taxi driver, used to travelers like me, grabbed my luggage with automatic gestures and set it down on the sidewalk in front of my future home. He smiled as he said goodbye and, without giving me time to respond, drove off.

I stood frozen in the middle of the street and took a couple of minutes to come back to reality; I couldn't stay there indefinitely. I grabbed my suitcases and, as best I could, climbed the stairs, weaving around the empty flowerpots, until I reached the porch. There was barely any room to move in that small entryway, which was full of empty planters and had a bench with cushions shoved into one corner. Everything looked faded. The wooden door, painted dark brown, looked old too. It had a small window with a curtain that must once have been white but was now yellowed. I looked for a doorbell in vain and decided to knock.

A few seconds later, a short, middle-aged man with round glasses and gray hair and beard opened the door. It was James, Aaron's father. Aaron appeared behind him. They helped me with my luggage and invited me inside.

That house looked like the home of an antique collector. It smelled damp and musty. Everything appeared worn, bearing the marks of time's relentless passage. Colorful Persian rugs of various patterns covered the creaking wooden floor. A half-finished partition separated the kitchen from the living room. Disorder reigned there, with items piled in every corner. Any surface was a good place to set down lamps, books, statues, unopened mail, keys… A patina of dust coated it all. It seemed as though they had intended to move things to their proper places, but that final step had never been taken.

Fortunately, although the kitchen was also quite old, it was much tidier and cleaner. There was a steaming pot and a bowl of salad, dinner was in the making. James stayed behind there, and Aaron showed me my room upstairs. It was decorated in an eclectic style, mixing furniture of different colors and designs. To my surprise, it had a terrace, but in keeping with the rest of the house, the floor was cracked and unusable. It wasn't the best room, but it would be sufficient to start.

"Anything you need, just let me know. I hope you feel at home. Here are towels in case you need them," Aaron said as he approached the door. "I'm going to help my father with dinner. Come down when you're ready."

"Thank you so much, Aaron. I'll take a shower and then come down," I said, smiling as I opened my suitcase.

My clothes were damp and cold. That sensation, as on other occasions, transported me back to Asturias for a few seconds. I sighed. I took a shower in that old-fashioned bathroom and went downstairs to dinner. I was exhausted, but I was also starving.

As a nod to their religion and culture, James had made *matzo balls* soup, a traditional Jewish dish. It was delicious, and I went back for seconds. It was a very pleasant dinner with no awkward silences. Aaron was cheerful and told me all about the neighborhood, about Baltimore, where to shop, the Saturday market… He made a real effort to share anything that might be useful to me.

James seemed reserved at first, but he soon opened up and, during dinner, told me the story of his Jewish ancestors. He had a glass eye that lent him a somewhat distant expression. He was endearing, and it was clear he was eager for company.

I was glad I had rented the room in that house; I felt comfortable and safe with them. I also liked Leo, their chubby brown cat. He would lie down beside us so we could pet him, and he ate the leftovers from James's dinner.

Among all the objects in that living room, a landline phone caught my attention most. It was vintage style with a rotary dial. I hadn't seen one like it in years. Far from being mere decoration, James used it to call his sister, who rang that very night.

After dinner, I went straight to bed. The room was cold. I put on my winter pajamas and curled up under the blanket on that bed with its cold purple sheets. There were no blinds, and the streetlight streamed through the window, casting the silhouettes of the furniture. Despite my exhaustion, it took me a while to fall asleep. I felt very alone and couldn't stop thinking about everything I had left behind. I was far from Spain, and it would be a long time before I returned. Now I had to fight to carve out a place for myself in this city, give my best at work, and make the most of the experience.

Those first weeks were tough, and when I got home in the evenings, loneliness would overtake me and I'd find myself crying. I missed Gijón and my mother's hug, the walks in the fine rain with my father, and the sunsets from my bedroom window. I missed simple everyday things like the grocery store in my neighborhood, where I could read the labels and knew the aisles and each product's location. I also longed for my mother's cooking, since I wasn't used to cooking and many nights I'd have a tuna sandwich for dinner just to keep things simple.

I was also having a hard time making friends and, aside from Aaron and James, I had no one to lean on. I spent too much time on the phone talking to my friends or my parents. Sometimes I called Daniel. His optimism was always a breath of fresh air, but deep down, the person I really wanted to talk to was Yazid. His voice wrapped me in calm, like a soft blanket against the night. It was hard to admit, but I couldn't help it, and I still felt an irresistible attraction to him.

Days went by, and little by little I got used to that new life and found my place. James and Aaron had become my family, and our bond grew stronger. They began sharing details of their lives, of their past. James had struggled with alcoholism, and because of it, his marriage had fallen apart. He'd been sober for a couple of years and now missed his wife more than he missed beer. He was somewhat socially isolated and worked two shifts as a waiter in two different restaurants to drown out the echo of his thoughts and escape loneliness. Aaron said it was his way of staying connected to the world. Many afternoons he brought home leftover food from the restaurant, which reminded me of Sam, one of my housemates in Cleveland.

Aaron and I got along well, and many nights we stayed up talking after dinner. One of our favorite routines was to walk to the neighborhood grocery store and buy a pint of chocolate ice cream. We'd sit on the faded bench at the entrance to eat it, chatting about past anecdotes or events from our day.

My job also gained meaning over time. It was a combination of examining patients and analyzing data. My boss had many active projects in which I collaborated. Multiple sclerosis was an enigma, and the more patients I examined, the more fascinated I became. It affected mostly young people and could present and progress in very different ways. I encountered patients in their sixties who barely had any symptoms, while others completely debilitated at thirty. It wasn't clear why this disease was so varied, and that intrigued me greatly.

Gradually I got the hang of the work and grew increasingly comfortable. Despite that, I still wondered how it was possible that they had hired me, a complete unknown with no experience, at one of the best hospitals in the world. Silently, I continued worrying that I wouldn't live up to expectations, but I knew that, with time, I would prove they'd made the right choice.

The first two months passed, and although I was very comfortable living with Aaron and James, the time had come for me to live on my own. Aaron had a pickup truck with a large trunk and helped me move to Mount Vernon. I had chosen that neighborhood because it was more central and had more restaurants and cafés. It was also safer than Charles Village and closer to the hospital.

The apartment was on the fourteenth floor of one of the tallest buildings in the neighborhood, with beautiful views of the Downtown skyline. It was quite small, with just one bedroom and a kitchen that doubled as a living room. It followed the typical American layout, with gray carpeted floors and a disproportionately large walk-in closet compared to the rest of the apartment.

As I unpacked and the place slowly started to feel like home, I found myself daydreaming about what it would be like if Yazid came to visit. Enjoying those views, that city, with him. I knew he was planning to come to the U.S. sometime in late summer, but I didn't know exactly when or where. He liked keeping things mysterious, and ever since I had moved to Baltimore, he had avoided the topic altogether.

One August afternoon, just when I least expected it, he broke the news.

"By the way, Lola, I know I've been dodging the topic for the past few months, but I didn't want to get my hopes up until the trip was confirmed. I had some issues with the visa," he said, his voice clearly full of emotion. "I've got a flight to Chicago in ten days."

"Seriously?" I hadn't seen that coming at all. "I'm so happy for you!"

"Yes, seriously. And, by the way, I haven't stopped thinking about how much I want to see you again," he added, his voice slightly trembling. "Would you want to come to Chicago? I think you guys have a national holiday that weekend."

"I don't even know what to say, I wasn't expecting this, but I'd love to see you," I replied, still in shock. After all his vague answers whenever I brought it up, I had ruled out the possibility of us meeting again so soon. "Let me check flight prices. I'm dying to see you too!"

And just like that, almost three years later, the fantasy of seeing each other again became reality. We hadn't talked about our expectations, or the conflicts from the past. The only thing that mattered was how much we wanted to be together. There were still so many feelings between us.

17

September 2, 2016

Chicago, Illinois, United States

The plane gradually lost altitude and circled over Chicago before landing. The city was massive, and its skyscrapers, bathed in the golden light of sunset, seemed to melt into the shoreline of Lake Michigan. The lake was so vast it blended into the horizon, it looked like an ocean. That view was stunning and served as the perfect welcome.

We finally touched down, and the plane slowed little by little. It hadn't even come to a complete stop when the sound of seatbelts being unbuckled began to fill the cabin. It was a special weekend, and you could feel everyone's impatience. Monday was Labor Day, a national holiday marking the unofficial end of summer in the U.S. Everyone wanted to make the most of the last warm days, and the airport was packed. Everywhere I looked, there were lines, some for passengers waiting to board, others for people trying to get served at fast food places, like the long line at McDonald's. The terminal smelled of pretzels and French fries. I was hungry.

As I made my way toward the exit, I couldn't stop thinking about what it would be like to see Yazid again. In just an hour, I would be face to face with him. A knot formed in my stomach, and my heart leapt into my throat, my hunger disappeared. I tried to calm myself down. There was still the cab ride to his place. Yazid wouldn't be picking me up. Yet, as I walked through the arrivals gate, I glanced around, just in case. A small part of me hoped he might surprise me. I felt a twinge of disappointment when I didn't see him there. Without thinking too much, I headed to the public transportation area and got a cab.

His house was about half an hour away, but the ride felt endless. I tried to distract myself with the scenery. I made small talk with the cab driver, but my nerves had taken over my mind, and I couldn't calm down. As the GPS counted down the remaining minutes, my heart raced faster and faster. How would the reunion go? How would we react? The chemistry between us was undeniable, but the uncertainty of what might happen that weekend made me anxious.

We exited the highway into a residential neighborhood. Most of the houses were two-story homes with a vintage feel. There were massive trees lining the streets and cars parked along both sides. It was already dark, and the lighting was dim. There were hardly any pedestrians. The taxi wound its way through side streets until we finally reached 1447 Berwyn Street. A chill ran down my spine. I got out with my backpack and took a deep breath. I had arrived.

I double-checked the address to make sure it was the right one and walked up the front steps. A faint light illuminated the entryway, which had clearly seen better days. Flyers stuck out of the mailbox, and a newspaper still wrapped in plastic lay forgotten on the floor. Everything gave off a sense of neglect. It was a building with several units, but I didn't know which one was Yazid's. I texted him to let him know I was there. The knot in my stomach tightened. A few minutes later, I heard hurried footsteps coming down the stairs. My pulse quickened again. It felt like anyone standing nearby could hear my heartbeat.

Yazid opened the door with a smile. Three years later, there we were. He reached out to shake my hand, but instinctively, I brushed it aside and hugged him. It felt like no time had passed. All the emotions buried by time and distance resurfaced in an instant. He stood frozen, but I heard a sigh escape him as we embraced. We stayed like that for a couple of minutes before finally reacting. We didn't say anything. He took my hand, and I followed him up the stairs to the second floor.

The apartment was dimly lit, but his room glowed with candles, casting a warm, amber light. He led me to his bed, and in silence, we lay down facing each other. His smile was wider than ever. His eyes sparkled into mine. For a few minutes, we just stared, not touching, as if we needed that moment to process that we were actually there, together. A few tears slipped down his cheeks. I let out a nervous laugh. I reached for his face and gently wiped his tears with my fingers. We closed the distance between us, undressing as we went. He held me, and I held him. My mind faded away with the touch of his skin. I kissed his neck, his scent hadn't changed.

We gave in to the longing and hunger that had built up since the last time. Dawn found us entwined, returning to each other the love that had been waiting. It was a feeling too complex to explain, perhaps it didn't need to be defined, only felt. Being apart from Yazid for so long had made me forget how intense my emotions were with him. When I was with him, I lost control of myself.

That weekend, I walked on air, seeing nothing beyond his eyes. It was like a mirage where, for a few days, we escaped reality, and the differences between us, the pain, the old wounds, the silence, the misunderstandings, the outsiders, and the void that had grown between us. We shut out all the problems and focused only on us. We walked the streets of Chicago like any couple, oblivious to the rest of the world. We hugged for any reason, kissed for no reason, laughed at everything, and just enjoyed each other's company. I could've lived in those days forever. In his presence, I found the comfort I so badly needed, so far from home.

However, not everything was rosy. On Sunday night, the last day before I was set to leave, the ghosts of the past slipped in through the window without mercy. It felt like Yazid had waited until the very last moment to bring it all up.

We were lying on his bed, after a nap that had stretched into the evening. It puzzled me that he had kept those feelings bottled up until the final day of the weekend.

"Lola, I'm sorry if I sound like a broken record. Now that I'm here with you, I realize that when I look at you, all those things you did that hurt me still come to mind," he admitted, turning to lie on his back and placing his arms behind his head. He avoided my gaze.

"Love, I don't really understand what this is about. I don't get why you can't just focus on the present. After all, that's all we really have. And in all this time, I've shown you how much I love you."

"I know… but I have a hard time letting go. I also keep thinking about how you got back with Daniel after you'd been with me. Did you never get over him? The more I think about it, the more it bothers me," he said, pausing between phrases. He was clearly struggling to find the right words.

"I don't know what you expect me to say. Daniel meant a lot to me, and it's easy to fall back into the past when someone's always treated you well. Sometimes I wish you could forgive me the way he did. I've shown you more than you've ever shown me, but you don't seem to see that," I replied, frustration creeping in as I realized we hadn't made any real progress.

"Everyone's different. I don't like being compared to anyone. I don't compare you to the girls in Jordan. You're all different, and you see the world, and behave, very differently," he sighed.

"So what do you want me to do with all these feelings you have?" I tried to keep my voice calm.

"I want to find a solution. Don't think I haven't been thinking about this for days. Sometimes it's hard for me to accept that you've been with other guys, and that you're so open-minded about relationships between men and women," he confessed, his voice tinged with frustration and something like desperation.

We talked until the early hours, going in circles over the same topics. I thought that if I just let him get it all out, everything that had hurt him in the past, even if it was the fourth time we were discussing it, maybe eventually he'd be able to leave that emotional baggage behind and move forward.

That night, Yazid opened Pandora's box and let out all the problems he had locked away, and I felt him drift into a space of pain and distance. His position stood in sharp contrast to mine. I didn't feel any bitterness toward him or toward what had happened between us. I didn't deny that Yazid had let me down with some of his past reactions and his lack of consistency in making future plans, but I had come to terms with reality. I just wanted us to focus on the present and enjoy it.

That night helped us realize that while time can give you perspective, it doesn't necessarily solve anything. It was clear that we loved each other and that, beyond physical attraction, there was a deep connection between us, but it would take much more than that to reconcile with our past. We decided to leave the conversation for another time and curled up under the sheets, falling asleep in each other's arms until dawn.

We had breakfast together, and Yazid accompanied me to the airport. We said goodbye with tight hugs, without any clear plan, but fully aware that we had a lot of work ahead, whatever our relationship was. He would be staying in the U.S. for several months, and in the meantime, we would try to work things out. With a little luck, we'd find a way to build a future together.

We parted ways at O'Hare Airport, with tears from my cheeks soaking into his shirt and a hug that lasted for several minutes. I hated saying goodbye to Yazid, it always felt like I was walking away from the love of my life. I hoped the day would come when I'd never have to say goodbye to him again.

On the plane ride back, I couldn't stop replaying everything that had happened that weekend. I kept thinking about how powerful the echoes of the past can be, how they sneak into the present and shape the future, no matter how much time goes by.

I began to understand the damage I had caused, to him, to myself, to us.

18

After that bittersweet weekend, the cycle of arrivals and goodbyes began. Some weekends I went to see him, and others, he came to visit me. Yazid traveled a lot, from coast to coast, always with work meetings. But weekends were free, and they were mine. Despite everything that had happened in the past, the moments we shared were always unforgettable, and time flew out the bedroom window as if it were made of minutes, not hours. When I was with him, I felt intoxicated, everything else faded into the background. In his eyes, I found the peace I had lost during his absence. I dreamed that one day these reunions would become something permanent, but so much still needed to change for that to happen. Neither of us knew how we were going to make it work.

Yazid swung from one extreme to the other in a heartbeat. We could be doing great, and suddenly, something would trigger a memory from the past, and everything would shift. These mood swings were usually followed by long conversations where we tried to make peace with the past. We both made an effort to communicate better and see things from each other's point of view. Our relationship was unstable, and we could go from heaven to hell, and back again, in a matter of five minutes. That unpredictability, that emotional roller coaster, made the relationship all the more addictive.

It took several of those conversations for me to start understanding his position. For me, it had been hard to stay true to my values and not move out of the house in Cleveland. But it had been hard for Yazid too. For starters, after what had happened between Daniel and me, he was incapable of trusting me blindly. His culture had not prepared him to accept women having so much freedom, and the fact that I shared an apartment with five strangers felt like a provocation to him. On top of that—and even though it happened after we had already broken up—it deeply bothered him that there had been a "part two" with Daniel. At first, he had acted indifferent, but now it was clear just how much it had affected him. He reproached me for how easily I had moved on, and worse, he kept insisting I had never really gotten over Daniel.

I could think of a thousand reasons to explain his anger or the issues we were having, but I didn't believe those reasons justified his lack of trust. It hurt that Yazid didn't seem to value all I had done to try and build a future with him, that his distrust kept him from seeing the bigger picture. No matter how hard I tried, things kept getting worse.

The last weekend of October, I went to visit him in Chicago. We had spent the whole day without leaving his bed. The sun had already set, and a couple of candles on the nightstand lit the room. Instrumental music with a Spanish guitar played softly in the background. We were curled up naked under the duvet, savoring the last few hours before I had to leave.

I was gently stroking his right arm while resting on his chest, eyes closed. The moment was perfect, until Yazid broke it with a proposal.

"Lola, I've been thinking… If we compare romantic or sexual experiences, you've been with more people than I have." He shared this thought like it was something he'd been carrying around for a long time.

"Yeah, but I don't really see where you're going with this. Does it even matter?" I didn't understand what he was trying to say.

"Well, maybe that's why I can't bring myself to trust you completely. Maybe that's why the past and the whole second chapter with Daniel bothers me so much."

"Honestly, I don't get it. The past is made of experiences, and that's where it belongs, in the past. What we have now is the present," I replied. I was beginning to sense where this was going, and it was making me nervous. "I don't understand your obsession with the past. We can't go on like this…"

Yazid gently moved my arm aside so he could turn and look me in the eye. I didn't know where to look, my cheeks were burning.

"What you don't understand is that, to me, you're mine. I don't want to think about other men being with you. I don't want to picture you with anyone else. Even if it happened before we met, it still bothers me. Knowing you were with Daniel after you were with me... that bothers me too. It makes me think you never really got over him." Yazid frowned as he said those last words.

"But I'm here with you. Isn't that enough?" I could hear the pain in his voice, but I couldn't understand it.

"No, it's not. I've only ever been with you, I don't know what it's like with other women. Maybe that's what I'm missing: perspective. Maybe if I sleep with someone else, I'll finally understand how you think, learn to trust you again, and make peace with this past that's haunting me," he confessed, releasing a long sigh as if the words had drained the tension from his body.

I didn't know what to say, it felt like madness, and it hurt that he wanted to be with other women. I couldn't relate to his point of view at all, much less to the logic behind that suggestion. I was convinced that all those reflections were just a way to justify his desire to explore and meet other women, while making me feel guilty at the same time. I saw him as manipulative, and the whole thing seemed absurd and unnecessary. I had shown him more love than I had ever shown anyone, and all my actions had always been directed toward building a future with him. Maybe his truth and mine were equally valid, but in that moment, neither of us could see things from the other's side.

After a few moments of silence, I gave in. I was too blinded by love, and the good times overshadowed the painful ones. If

Yazid wanted to try being with other women, so be it. I still hoped he would come to his senses and we could move past these ridiculous conflicts. But I had no idea how I was going to handle the jealousy.

"If that's what you want, fine, go ahead. But do you really believe that being with other women will help you trust me?" I paused. "I don't understand your logic. I think it's only going to make things worse, but if that's what you want, fine."
What I was agreeing to went against my values, and it was hard to even say those words. Out of love, I was compromising too much.
"Are you sure?" he asked, surprised.

"I don't know if I can handle it, but you're not giving me any other option. What I want is to be okay with you." As I said the words, I knew I was betraying myself.

It wasn't hard for Yazid to start seeing other women. He was attractive and charming, he had plenty of opportunities. Sometimes I was curious and would ask about the girls, wanting to know who they were or see pictures. Other times, I was afraid I'd compare myself to them and come out losing. He never told me what actually happened, but he insisted on sharing details about their looks or personalities, almost as if he enjoyed the pain it caused me. I had never been the jealous type, but I became insecure, seeing a threat in every woman we passed. He kept repeating that he was doing it for us, but I couldn't understand his reasoning.

The situation made no sense and was slowly destroying what was left of my fragile self-esteem. I didn't know how to stop it. I

167

tried to believe him, to convince myself that these experiences were somehow good for both of us, but the self-deception never lasted long. When we weren't together and he took a long time to reply or didn't answer his phone, I imagined the worst and felt miserable. Yes, I had been with other guys in the past, but never while I was with him. Yazid, on the other hand, had the option to be with me, and chose to be with others. He acted coldly. His behavior made me feel like I didn't really know him, like his mind worked in twisted ways.

The situation was overwhelming me. I was far from my sister and my friends, and too ashamed to share what I was going through. So I decided to say nothing and suffer in silence.

I felt like I was losing him a little more with each new girl he dated, and it became harder and harder to say goodbye at the end of each weekend. Our relationship had deteriorated into a power struggle. Yazid controlled the situation however he pleased, sometimes disappearing for days, then suddenly smothering me with affection and treating me like a queen. That extreme behavior confused me. Every time I felt like I couldn't take it anymore, Yazid would show up as if nothing had happened and lift me to the clouds with his love. He gave me exactly the affection I needed at the exact moment I needed it, making it impossible for me to walk away.

I couldn't take it anymore. Finally, one day, I gathered the strength to end it. I knew I wouldn't be able to stay true to myself if we spoke in person, so I took advantage of one of our midweek phone calls.

"Yazid, either you stop seeing other women or we're done. I can't take this anymore," I said, without preamble, without pause. I tried to stay calm.

"Lola, I don't enjoy any of this, and I never see the same girl twice," he said, barely raising his voice. "Like I've told you a hundred times, I'm doing this for us."

"I'm sorry, but I can't do it anymore. When are you going to stop?"

"You're right." He paused. "If you don't want me to, I won't do it anymore."

"Please... I'm at rock bottom."

"I'm really sorry," he said. "That was never my intention, not even close. But I had to do it so we could move forward." "You know my insecurities better than anyone. No matter how much you say you're doing this for us, you're the one who's been ignoring my feelings."

I sighed. It seemed like Yazid was finally starting to see reason. What I didn't know was how we were going to repair the damage his actions had done to our relationship. He had been incredibly selfish. But it didn't end there, Yazid still had something else to say.

"By the way, Lola, there's something else I want you to know."

"Go ahead. At this point, I don't know what to expect from you," I replied sarcastically, trying to hide how afraid I was of another unpleasant surprise.

"Nothing ever happened with those girls," he admitted.

"Wait, I don't get it. Then why were you going out with them?"

"During those dates, I never went beyond small talk. The only thing I wanted was for you to put yourself in my shoes," he admitted. He paused again. "I wanted you to feel what I felt when you lived with all those strangers in Cleveland… or when I found out you had gotten back together with Daniel."

We fell silent. With that confession, Yazid revealed just how twisted his mind could be. He hadn't wanted me to empathize, he had wanted to hurt me.

"I don't know what bothers me more," I said, "that you were with other women, or that you made me believe you were, when you weren't. All just so I'd feel what you felt back then. You never cease to surprise me."

Our relationship was becoming more toxic by the day. I no longer knew what to do. Sometimes I was afraid of how his mind worked. Things had stopped making sense a long time ago.

"Lola…"

"To me, this is nothing but revenge," I cut him off. "Instead of making things better, you've only made them worse," I told him. "What hurts the most is that you knew exactly how much you were hurting me, and still, you made me believe you were involved with other girls. I never did anything like that to you."

"I was trying to get you to see things from my perspective, so you'd understand what I went through," he insisted.

"And did it help? Because I still think you did it just to get back at me."

"I'm sorry. Maybe it wasn't the smartest idea," he admitted. "I thought that if you understood, you wouldn't do it again. That gives me peace of mind for our future. But you're right, things got out of hand."

"Some days, I feel like I don't know you at all. I struggle to make sense of how you think."

That behavior from Yazid was one more thorn in our already damaged relationship, weakening it further. We kept seeing each other and spending time together, but it wasn't the same anymore. Everything felt poisoned. I wished I could go back to those days in Amman, when we didn't have any problems between us.

Sometimes I couldn't even tell the difference between loving him and hating him. A part of me kept saying I should run away. He had hurt me so much, but whether he meant to or not, I still couldn't walk away from him. Especially now that we were in the same country and, after all this time, we could finally be together. Naively, I still dreamed of the day when everything would finally fall into place.

19

I ignored his messages and refused to see him for two weeks. I kept replaying our last conversation in my head. It was incredibly hard to forgive his behavior, and even harder to accept the intentions behind it. I would have preferred he hadn't been so convoluted. If he had simply admitted to sleeping with those women to gain the "perspective" he said he needed, rather than pretending to hurt me on purpose, it would've been easier to process.

That supposed polygamy had been pure torture for me. I was still deeply hurt, but it didn't take long before I found myself desperately missing him. Yazid was my weakness. No matter how many reasons or arguments I had to be angry, all he had to do was say he loved me and throw in a few sweet words, and I would lose all sense and forget everything that had happened.

We saw each other again on a Friday at the end of January. A cold wave had swept across the country, and in Baltimore, the temperatures hadn't risen above freezing. It had snowed all day, and the situation was even worse in Chicago, several flights had been canceled. Fortunately, Yazid's wasn't; he was scheduled to arrive around eight that evening. I couldn't wait to hold him.

I wanted everything to be perfect. I left work early to prepare the apartment and cook his favorite dish: *shorbet adas*, a lentil soup. A couple of months earlier, we'd had it at an Arab restaurant in town called Zaatar. He'd loved it so much that a few days later I went back to get the recipe. Yazid adored that soup and said it reminded him of his grandmother's.

My cousin always said that cooking when your partner gets home is essential, that every man, whether he realizes it or not, is looking for a sense of home, and the smell of food helps create it. She claimed those sensations reach the subconscious and draw him in before he even knows it. It might be considered manipulative, but to me, it was just another tool to win him over. I followed her advice religiously.

As expected, due to the snowstorm, Yazid's flight was delayed. Around eleven that night, he texted to say he was about to land. I went down to the door to wait for him, full of anticipation. I had touched up my makeup from that morning and wore a green lingerie set under my clothes, something I had bought just for him. The excitement of seeing him again wiped away every bad feeling.

He pulled up in a yellow cab and stepped out with that irresistible smile. He wore his black wool coat, a gray wool scarf, and leather gloves. We hugged, and I lost myself in his scent.

174

"I missed you, Lola," he whispered in my ear. "I've been longing to feel your skin for far too many days."

"And I missed you…" I melted into his arms and tried not to think about the reason I had avoided him for the past two weeks.

As soon as the elevator doors closed, he hugged me again. Still holding each other, we walked down the hallway to my door. Just as I'd hoped, he loved the smell of food in the apartment. He took a shower, and after dinner, we headed to the bedroom to be with each other.

Despite all the hurt, I couldn't deny how much I enjoyed his company. In those moments, it felt easier to forget the past and live in the present. That was better than missing him and suffering through his absence. Still, the truce didn't last long. The next morning, with daylight beginning to seep in and me still half asleep, Yazid told me the date of his return to Jordan.

"Baby, I waited until I could tell you in person, I'm leaving next Friday," he said, breaking the silence and the peace in the room. "My meetings wrap up this month."

"You're kidding… so soon?" I knew this moment would come eventually, but I hadn't imagined it would be so soon.

"Love," he whispered, trying to soften the blow, "I told you I wouldn't stay more than five or six months." He ran his fingers through my hair.

I buried my face in his chest and cried. Just thinking about it made me miss him already. I was scared of the future, especially of what it meant for our relationship: we had more than enough problems and not nearly enough long-term plans. Distance wouldn't help, and time was working against us.

"Why didn't you tell me sooner? Please, postpone the flight," I begged, forcing the words out, trying to regain some control.

"As soon as I'm done here, I have to fly to Riyadh to meet with my father and some clients. Things are going really well, and if we're lucky, we'll close a big contract with the suppliers of our flagship product," he explained, gently stroking my cheek.

"Yazid, I don't understand your business world, let alone why you've abandoned your passion for medicine." It was a topic we'd long avoided.

"What do you mean?" he asked, surprised. "These meetings are for selling medical devices and instruments on a large scale. It's less demanding than being a medical resident, my dad pays me much better, and I don't feel like a slave to the system."

"I get your point, but you know residency is temporary. Once you finish and become a specialist, the work is better paid and less stressful. If you stay in this business, your life will be based in the Middle East. But if you became a doctor here, we could actually have a future together." I couldn't bring myself to accept his logic.

That weekend would be the last we'd spend together. I was still recovering from our last fight, and this felt like a bucket of ice-cold water. A thousand scenarios played out in my head, and they all ended with us apart. I'd have to wait for a vacation to see him again or for him to return to the United States, and we'd always be at the mercy of circumstances. I had no control over any of it.

"Please don't take that flight. You can stay here with me while you study for the two exams you have left to complete your residency," I insisted once more. "That way, we could both pursue our dream and be together."

"Lola, my dreams are different now, and you know it. I have a much better idea."

"Tell me." He kissed me on the cheek, his lips damp with my tears.

"Why don't you come with me to Amman? You'd have everything there, we'd be together; you could learn Arabic and even do your neurology residency."

"Are you kidding me?" I blurted out before he could finish. A nervous laugh of disbelief escaped me. "After all the work and study I've put into being here and making a name for myself in this country, you come to me with this? Do you realize I started all of this for you?" I went from sadness to frustration.

"Things have changed."

"I keep my word, unlike you."

"Lola, things aren't as you think."

"Really? I'm sorry, but now it's too late to turn back." My mouth was dry and my heart was racing. "Besides, you know it would be much harder to advance my career in Jordan."

I got up to get a glass of water, and that ended the conversation. Neither he nor I would give up our professional futures, and they lay on different continents. We had to accept it: if things stayed this way, we were destined to live apart.

That weekend, we did everything we could to make the most of our time together. Neither he nor I knew when we'd see each other again. Once more, uncertainty and instability crept in, when would I see him next, let alone what might happen between us?

It didn't stop snowing all weekend. With his departure looming, we spent almost the entire time loving one another. We both felt an irresistible need for constant skin-to-skin contact. It was like a force beyond our control.

Yazid had that ability to make time fly, and Sunday arrived almost without my realizing it. I felt dizzy at the thought that it might be our last night together. I didn't want to think about Monday morning, when he'd head back to Chicago. I wished for a storm, for it to keep snowing, and for him to stay with me all week. Instead, Monday morning brought sunshine. The snowplows had cleared the streets, ready for the week ahead.

The alarm marked the end of the night and, with it, a reality we could no longer ignore. It was seven in the morning, and his flight left at ten. I resisted beneath the sheets, but we didn't have much time left. Yazid held me tightly and kissed my neck, trailing down to my shoulders. I loved it when he did that. With my eyes still closed, I turned toward him and kissed him back.

That Monday would be the hardest and the coldest morning of the entire winter. Parting from him without knowing when I'd see him again was truly agonizing. As we waited for the taxi, Yazid held me close and I buried my face in his chest. Neither of us knew that those would be our last moments together for a long time.

"I'll miss you, Lola," he said, looking at me. "These months in the United States haven't been easy, but I want you to know one thing: I love you."

"And I love you, too." I hugged him tighter. "I'll see you soon, promise?"

He got into the taxi and disappeared down the street among the cars. I stood there, my gaze fixed on the passing vehicles as I reflected on us.

Things had changed a lot since our first goodbye at the Amman airport. Almost four years had passed, and we were no longer the same. Our relationship had evolved too, and now we were a couple trying to save something already falling apart. We still had no plan for our future together and, worse yet, neither he nor I knew how we were going to find one.

That farewell could have been the perfect moment to walk away from him and free myself from that dysfunctional relationship, but I chose to keep trying. His ideas clashed with mine, and his happiness would cost me mine, and vice versa. Despite everything, I kept fighting for a future with him, crashing against the same wall time and time again.

20

I grew accustomed once more to days without his laughter, to weekends without him, and to solitude. Time passed, and I clung to the hope of seeing him again in April, even though I had no real certainty it would happen. I retreated into my own world to cope with his absence, fantasizing about seeing him again and falling asleep in his arms.

I dreamed that one day things might change, but neither of us was willing to give in. Yazid remained focused on his obligations to the family business and was determined not to disappoint his father. His life revolved around those meetings, wherever in the world they took him. I, on the other hand, was convinced the United States was where I belonged and that my education was paramount. Sacrificing my professional future for love was a price I wasn't willing to pay.

Moreover, his behavior over the past few months had only underscored the risk I'd face if I gave it all up for him. I often asked myself why I would stay in such a situation when I could probably find a European or American man, someone whose values aligned more closely with mine and who would make my life easier.

I filled the void Yazid left when he returned to the Middle East by throwing myself into work and taking on new projects. I took great pleasure in my work, and it helped me escape everything. Both my boss and the rest of the team were very pleased with my dedication, but as the workload grew exponentially, I sometimes felt overwhelmed.

In addition to performing neurological exams on patients with multiple sclerosis, I also conducted optical coherence tomography scans, two-dimensional images of the retina used to measure its thickness. Those scans were crucial, because by analyzing retinal thickness one could infer whether there was inflammation or degeneration in the brain. My boss used to say that the eyes, as well as being the window to the soul, were also windows to the brain, and that the healthier the retina, the healthier the brain.

All of these concepts were new to me, and the more I learned and understood them, the more fascinated I became with that field of medicine. I found it incredibly inspiring to see how technology advanced our understanding of such a devastating disease. Through our research, we contributed to the scientific community, and being part of that made me feel fulfilled.

Fortunately, life wasn't all work. I also began to rebuild my social life. I reconnected with Aaron and James, who were thrilled to see me again. I started meeting up with a group of Spaniards

I'd met during my first days at Johns Hopkins. Many of them were researchers too. They'd been in the city for a couple of years and had formed a tight-knit circle. On weekends, they'd gather for drinks at someone's apartment and then head out to party in Fells Point, the city's oldest neighborhood. They didn't follow American schedules, meetings would start late, "Spanish time." After the bars closed, the party often continued right where it began. Although they seemed happy so far from Spain, they hadn't fully integrated into American society and sometimes felt isolated. I enjoyed their company, but I preferred smaller gatherings, large groups tended to keep conversations superficial and blur individual personalities.

Luckily, I connected with one woman in the group. We began meeting one-on-one, and she became my main support and confidante in the city. Her name was Amaya, she was two years older than me, from San Sebastián, and was pursuing a PhD in biochemistry at Johns Hopkins University. She lived two blocks from my apartment, and on weekday afternoons we'd walk together from Mount Vernon to Bolton Hill. We talked about everything, from our romantic struggles to our longing to return to Spain, and compared life in the U.S. with life back home.

Before moving to Baltimore, we had both viewed the United States as one of the most advanced countries in the world. But after a few months here, we discovered how deceptive appearances could be. The country had many shortcomings and deep inequalities, and Baltimore was a perfect example. The city suffered from racial segregation and lacked basic rights like access to quality education and healthcare. Johns Hopkins Hospital, one of the best in the country and internationally renowned, sat in one of the city's poorest neighborhoods, surrounded by people who were socially and economically marginalized. Amaya and I saw things the same way. Talking with her about these issues was therapeutic and helped me make sense of it all.

In addition to Amaya, I became close friends with Afsaneh. I'd met her through a girl at one of the Spaniards' gatherings, and we hit it off immediately. She was Iranian and had been in the U.S. for nearly ten years. After earning a master's in business, she now worked as a consultant at Deloitte. Although she'd already obtained U.S. citizenship, she hadn't lost her roots or her accent, and she still missed Iran. She was five years my senior and often offered me advice about Baltimore and life in general. Sometimes I saw her as an older sister.

Amaya and Afsaneh were instrumental in helping me endure Yazid's absence. I also leaned on Aaron and other coworkers, most of whom were expatriates. Between us there was a special bond, an unspoken language that didn't exist with Americans. After all, we were far from home, and only fellow immigrants could truly understand our challenges and shared experiences.

While I was building my social circle in Baltimore, my relationship with Yazid continued to deteriorate. The unresolved issues and unanswered questions from our past wore it down. The final straw came in April, when I changed my plans. I had a couple of weeks off, and Yazid and I had talked about seeing each other. That very month, my boss offered me the chance to work directly with the head of the Neurology Department, the most important figure in the entire division. He was a nationally recognized doctor with a great deal of influence. Getting a recommendation letter from him was crucial, perhaps even more valuable than my research experience at Johns Hopkins.

I felt cornered. It was a tough decision, but in the end, I couldn't turn down the opportunity. I decided to stay in Baltimore and take the rotation. Instead of supporting me, Yazid took it as a shift in priorities, even though he had never prioritized me. He got upset, and after that conversation, everything changed. Our calls became infrequent, and when we did talk, they were full of resentment. I felt trapped. Part of me missed him, but another part knew he wasn't good for me. Yazid had stopped being a source of support months earlier and had become an emotional burden. He drained my energy and made me feel guilty for everything that wasn't working in our relationship.

The thread grew more strained each day, until one Saturday morning, during one of our calls, Yazid finally snapped it.

"Lola, do you ever want to have kids someday?"

"Of course I do. Why are you asking? Do you want kids?"

"I do. I've never told you this, but I'd like to have ten. A big family. What do you think?"

"Come on, Yazid. You're joking, right?" I replied, stunned. This was just what we were missing. "Who has that many kids these days? Not even your grandparents or mine had that many. It's insane. Unless we're millionaires, I'd be a slave to the house. That's way too much work!"

"You're absolutely right, but it's something I've always dreamed of."

"Yazid, I'm sorry to say, but that's just not realistic. At least not with me. Think about it. How many women have that many kids? Do you know what pregnancy does to their bodies?" I was starting to get angry, it felt surreal. "There's just no need."

"I have a solution for that…" he said, trailing off dramatically.

"Okay, surprise me. Do you want to adopt? If that's your dream, maybe we could consider it," I said, already giving in again. "But I don't know what kind of relationship you could build with that many children. Honestly, it sounds exhausting. They'd end up raising each other. Wouldn't it make more sense to start with one and take it from there?"

"No, that's not the solution. I want to be the biological father of all of them," he said, his tone growing more serious.

"So then?" I braced myself.

"Well, look, if you think it's too much for you, I could marry more than one woman. That way the work would be divided."

"Yazid, for God's sake!" I thought he was kidding and let out a nervous laugh. "Why are you like this? First it was your whole thing about not making peace with the past, and now you want ten kids. Of course, what better way to get them than by marrying multiple women?"

"Lola, you have to respect my wishes."

"You talk about women as if we were objects, like we're just here to give birth," I snapped.

I paced around the living room as I spoke, trying not to lose my temper, trying to understand where Yazid was coming from. I refused to believe he meant it. I thought he was saying all this just to push me away. When I had been in Amman, it had seemed like polygamy was no longer practiced. I thought marrying more than one woman was a thing of the past, maybe still seen in remote villages or very conservative countries, but rare in modern cities and progressive societies like Jordan. Women's roles had been changing for years.

"Why do you always have to complicate things? I'm starting to think you're doing this just to drive me away." I struggled to put my thoughts into words. "No one in your family has more than one wife. Look at your parents, your brothers, your friends!"

"Lola, the Quran says we're allowed to have up to four wives. It's in the holy book…"

"Since when do you follow the Quran so literally? You sound like one of those stereotypical Arab men in movies or on the news, someone I never thought you were."

"I'm sorry, but that's what I want. And I don't think it's fair for you to force me to give up my desires. Ideally, we would both get what we want. You'd always be the first."

"Right. The first while you sleep with the others."

The conversation was spiraling. His attitude struck me as selfish. I felt like I was talking to a stranger. I couldn't understand his perspective. I refused to accept that being Muslim gave him a free pass to have a harem of wives and enough kids to start a soccer team. I knew that kind of thinking wasn't common. None of the Jordanians I had met held those beliefs. Not his father, not his uncles, no one had more than one wife.

"Lola, I want you. You have to understand where I'm coming from. To me, marriage is just a contract, a means to an end. With you, I have love, a romantic relationship. With the others, I'd only have children."

"Yazid, no. I refuse to be part of that plan. Look, I thought you were the love of my life, but the more I get to know you, the more like a stranger you seem."

"I'm sorry. But that's my dream… You need to open your mind, Lola."

"Seriously? No, thank you. This has gone way too far, and it's partly my fault for being so flexible with your irrational requests. I've had enough. It's over."

I had reached my limit. I gave up, there was nothing else I could do. I couldn't carry the weight of that relationship anymore, and if I didn't let it go, it was going to bury me. On May 2nd, I decided to walk away from that toxic relationship. We stopped talking. Silence fell between us.

21

Breaking up with Yazid lifted a weight off my shoulders I hadn't even realized I was carrying. I could finally rest from fighting for an impossible love. But it wasn't all peace, along with the relief came a sense of failure. I had been obsessed with making our relationship work for far too long, and now it was hard to accept the reality.

Not hearing from Yazid was difficult to handle. I was so used to his voice that I found myself thinking about him day and night, constantly fighting the temptation to call or message him. Reaching out was literally at my fingertips, just a quick click away. Choosing not to do it was an active decision, a constant internal struggle. Obsessed, I couldn't stop wondering whether he missed me too, or if, on the contrary, he had already started searching for the first of his four wives.

It took me at least a couple of weeks to process what had happened. I leaned on Afsaneh and Amaya, who patiently listened and supported me through my darkest days. I was embarrassed to say out loud what had finally triggered the end of our relationship. It was hard to tell them the whole truth.

"Lola, that's insane," Afsaneh exclaimed, stunned.

"You did the right thing. You've put up with way too much. It's just not worth it, seriously. You're amazing, sweetheart," Amaya added.

"I don't know. It's been really hard. I still can't believe it—but he said it so firmly..." The more I thought about it, the more it hurt. "I'm telling you, none of the Jordanians I met, none of their relatives, had more than one wife. Just my luck to fall in love with one of the few Arabs with backward ideas."

"I honestly think he said it to push you away. Look, in Iran, most people are Muslim too, and I don't know a single man who has more than one wife. That's something women stopped tolerating years ago. Maybe our great-great-grandparents..." Afsaneh tried to comfort me.

"I know it's hard to open your eyes, but better late than never. Thank God you didn't leave Baltimore to go live with him in Jordan," Amaya said, worried. "Can you imagine giving everything up to be with him, and then he hits you with that?"

We talked for a long time, and that conversation helped pull me out of my thoughts and made me feel understood. I was incredibly lucky to be able to trust them with something so personal and not feel judged.

Following their advice, I made a list on a piece of paper of all the reasons I had to walk away from him. I was surprised to find more than I expected. That simple act helped me realize that our relationship had been more toxic than I thought and reminded me of all the red flags I had been ignoring. I kept that piece of paper in my nightstand, and whenever I missed Yazid too much, I'd read it out loud. It filled me with anger and pain, but it reminded me why we weren't together anymore, and for a moment, it helped me stop longing for him.

The days grew longer and warmer, welcoming the arrival of summer. It was hard to believe, but I had already been in the country for over a year. I looked back and reflected on everything that had happened, the good and the bad. I felt proud of myself for getting through a year full of personal and professional challenges. Adjusting to life in the U.S. and making the decision to end my relationship with Yazid were two of the hardest things I had ever done.

The emotional toll had been significant, and although I was slowly recovering, I still felt drained. All I wanted was to rest and be surrounded by the people I loved. The feeling of uprootedness was still very present, and I dreamed of taking a vacation in Spain where I could truly recharge. Besides, I was applying for the Neurology residency that fall and knew it would be a long and stressful process.

I needed a break, a few days with my family and my people to regain strength. As soon as I found out that my boss would be on vacation in August and that many clinics would be closed, I requested two weeks off to go to Gijón.

The countdown to my trip to Spain felt slow. I tried to stay focused at work and push my projects forward so I wouldn't have to deal with them during the break, but my mind was fixated on landing in Madrid. I was beyond excited about the trip and everything I would do there. My thoughts were in Gijón, and every conversation seemed to revolve around the visit. My mom kept asking what I wanted her to cook, and when I spoke with my friends, instead of catching up, we made plans for when I got back. I felt special and lucky to have them. Gijón was my home, and despite the distance, I had family and friends waiting for me with open arms. After all, I had spent twenty-four years in that city. I was deeply connected to it.

That sense of rootedness is what, in my opinion, sets Spaniards apart from Americans. Based on conversations I'd had, it seemed like Americans didn't have such deep roots. Their social circles were much smaller than ours. For instance, when I asked my American friends about their origins, many told me they had lived in several different states and, even if they had grown up in one place, they had moved away so long ago that they no longer felt a connection to it. They moved around the country a lot, and maintaining long-term relationships seemed difficult. Very few of them still kept in touch with their childhood or teenage friends, something I couldn't even imagine. My girlfriends had been in my life for more than ten years.

The day of the flight finally arrived. It had been a long time since I was this excited to get on a plane. I didn't care about the seven-and-a-half-hour journey. I closed my suitcase and brought it to the door. I watered the plants and took out the trash before leaving. As I rode the elevator down, I double-checked that I had my passport and phone charger, the only essentials.

In a rush to get there, I headed for the airport. I arrived a couple of hours early. After checking in, I sat down in front of the boarding gate. I opened my laptop to answer some emails and finish a couple of work reports, but I got distracted by the passengers arriving and didn't make progress on either. People-watching was too entertaining. Many of them seemed to be Spanish, which made me feel even closer to home. I imagined the stories behind them. Maybe some were coming back from vacation, while others, like me, lived in the U.S. and were visiting family. You could see the joy on their faces, and they created that unmistakable Spanish buzz I missed so much.

Just like we Spaniards had a different relationship with our roots, we also related to others in a different way. We were much more spontaneous and social. We loved talking about our lives, and we commented on others' without hesitation. Americans, on the other hand, were far more reserved and independent; their personal lives were much more private, and gossip didn't have the same place it did with us.

The flight to Madrid felt shorter than expected. I was lucky to get a window seat, and with my pillow resting against the cabin wall, I managed to sleep for several hours. I was exhausted. A flight attendant woke me up for breakfast service. There were only two hours left. My heart started to race, I was so excited.

We landed in Barajas just as the sun was rising. I got off the plane and followed the signs to transfer from terminal T4S to T4. Before catching the bus to Gijón, I stopped to have Iberian ham sandwich with a coffee with milk at one of the cafés in the terminal. I recognized several fellow passengers from my flight.

It was clear the place catered to Spaniards abroad, missing a taste of home. I guess we all longed for those flavors that made us feel at home.

After a long journey, I arrived in Gijón on August 4th. It was a Friday afternoon. As I stepped off the bus, I breathed in the scent of the sea, the one only visitors can truly notice. The sky was gray, and a fine drizzle, typical of Asturias and known as *orbayu*, was falling. It didn't matter what time of year it was. When *orbayu* arrived, it could stay for days, even weeks.

I spotted my father waiting for me on the sidewalk. His face lit up when he saw me, and he ran to hug me. My mom and sister were waiting at home. I hadn't seen them in months, and now that they were close, I realized just how much I had missed them. Coming back to Gijón felt like reconnecting with my past self, with who I was and where I came from. It reaffirmed my identity. It gave me peace to know that this was still my place.

As was tradition, even without a birthday to celebrate, we had a family barbecue that Sunday to mark the fact that we were all together and that it was summer. My mother, a wonderful cook, prepared a feast with everyone's help, what my dad would call "next-level food." After living abroad, I had come to appreciate those dishes even more, things I simply couldn't find in the U.S. For a moment, I looked around at the table, which was overflowing with food, and I felt so lucky to be there.

It was fascinating to see how much my perspective had changed. I now valued things I once took for granted. I saw my parents differently, too. My mom, despite her limitations and how tabloid news sometimes filled her head with paranoid worries, was all heart, she always put us first. She had an incredible kindness, and her boundless love filled the whole house. My dad showed his love in a different way. He wasn't big on displays of affection, but he was always there to help and to offer thoughtful advice. He loved going on walks, and my sister and I enjoyed walking with him. Whether through the mountains or along the boardwalk, each of us linked to one of his arms, talking about relationships or life. Spending time with them again made me realize how many moments I was missing by living abroad. I felt a little guilty. I knew life was quietly slipping by. Just as I was becoming an adult woman, they were growing older.

During my visit, I also got to spend time with my friends, whom I had missed terribly. One of my favorite plans was to go to the *Cuesta del Cholo*, a sloped cobblestone street at the edge of Cimadevilla, right by the marina. The area was full of bars, and people would buy drinks, usually cider, and sit out on the street to drink and socialize. It was always crowded in the afternoons and was the perfect place to see and be seen. Gijón was small, and most of us made similar plans.

We went to *El Cholo* on a Thursday afternoon. It was a scorcher of a summer day, clear skies, not a single breeze. I had spent the day at La Ñora beach with my sister and two of my best friends from volleyball, Rebeca and Ana. To wrap up the day, we headed there for a drink. I wasn't dressed up, just wearing a pink dress from three summers ago, my hair wavy from the saltwater, and sand still clinging to my ankles. But I didn't care, with my tanned skin, I felt like everything looked good on me. We bought

195

a couple of bottles of cider and sat on a section of the wall, talking about our lives and enjoying the sunset.

The sun was setting, and night was falling. We were on our fourth bottle, and the alcohol was starting to kick in. Cider had this unique effect: It gave you a light buzz, made you laugh and feel spontaneous in a way no other drink could. I felt slightly tipsy, but at peace with life. When I compared the plans I made in the U.S. with the ones I made here, not even the fanciest restaurant could compete with a simple evening like this in Gijón. What was once ordinary had become extraordinary.

I was pouring cider for Rebeca when a guy on a bike rode past us at a decent speed. I caught a glimpse of him from the side but didn't pay much attention. My sister, who had drunk far less cider than I had, recognized Daniel and called out his name. He stopped to say hi with his usual easygoing charm. It had been a long time since we last talked. Our relationship had gone cold and eventually faded into silence months earlier, when I started replying to his messages days or even weeks late, out of fear that Yazid might read them and get the wrong idea.

I was genuinely happy to see him again, and judging by his smile, it seemed like he was happy to see me too. Daniel looked as attractive as ever, his skin was deeply tanned, and his beard and curls were just the same. He got off his bike and stayed for a bit to chat with us.

"Hey, girls! How's it going?" he asked casually. "Lola, I wasn't expecting to see you around here! I'm guessing you're visiting? Are you staying long?"

"Yeah, just here enjoying the summer and Gijón. I'll be heading back in about two weeks." I was a bit tense, and the cider wasn't helping, I kept stumbling over my words.

"That's great! I'm glad to hear it." He held my gaze for a few seconds. "Things are good here. I'm teaching diving classes now in Candás and at other beaches. I also bought a camper van for more freedom, you know..." He smiled as he shared his updates. "And I've been trying to break into design, I work from home now."

"So many changes! I'm really happy for you. That's what you always wanted, isn't it?"

For a moment, I imagined what my life might have looked like if we were still together.

"Yeah, it is! I feel really lucky. Well, I should get going... But if you have time for a drink sometime, text me. I'm really curious to hear about your adventures in Baltimore!" He smiled again and held my gaze once more. "See you later, girls!"

Despite the time that had passed and the fact that our relationship hadn't worked out, I still felt a strong attraction to him. There was a kind of unspoken communication between us, a sense of connection. I felt at ease around him.

My relationship with Yazid and the one I'd had with Daniel had been completely different. At first, I had valued my relationship with Yazid more, but now I realized that Daniel was a much more transparent, straightforward person, ultimately, a better fit for me. I was really glad I'd seen him again, and I took his suggestion to meet up seriously.

I wanted to enjoy his company, and after all, I was free to do as I pleased. I didn't care what Yazid might think anymore. He was no longer a part of my life.

22

Three days after running into Daniel, I sent him a message and we agreed to meet that very afternoon. I wondered whether it was a coincidence that he didn't already have plans, or if he had actually prioritized seeing me. We set a time around six in the evening to go for a bike ride. In a nod to the past, Daniel suggested meeting by the statue of Pelayo.

I knew nostalgia played a part, but I was genuinely excited to see him. I caught myself worrying about what to wear, shaving my legs, and choosing my underwear. I guess it's always better to be prepared for anything, but those actions hinted at my expectations. After several rounds pacing around my room, I settled on denim shorts, a white T-shirt, and a khaki green blazer. I wanted to look good for him, and I knew he loved that color. That afternoon the sky was overcast, but it was still warm. I rode my bike downtown. I was going faster than I should've, but I knew the streets like the back of my hand, and I was running late. I felt a flutter in my stomach that grew stronger as I got closer to our meeting spot.

Daniel was waiting, sitting by the fountain with his bike propped up next to him. He jumped up as soon as he saw me. His eyes were shining, and he was smiling. We greeted each other with a hug that lasted several seconds. He felt just as familiar as ever, as if no time had passed.

We walked our bikes through the crowd as we talked. The town square was packed, and riding there would've meant risking running someone over. Once we got to the Church of San Pedro, we hopped on our bikes and rode the rest of the way to Rinconín. The bike lane was narrow and full of traffic, so we had to go single file. Daniel rode in front and would occasionally turn around to make sure I was keeping up.

The pedestrian area was crowded too. There were people of all kinds: some enjoying the view or the calm evening, others out exercising, groups of teens just leaving the beach, retirees on benches, families with kids running around, barefoot surfers carrying their boards, neighbors walking their dogs, and tourists snapping photos nonstop. The promenade was a gathering place, one of the busiest and most beloved spots in the city.

We reached the end of the path, at Rinconín Park. That was my favorite place in all of Gijón. It was full of palm trees and home to the statue of the *Madre del Emigrante,* a monument created to honor Asturian emigrants and their mothers. Facing the sea, one arm outstretched, the figure represented a mother saying goodbye to her children who had set off for the Americas in search of fortune, vanishing into the horizon of the sea, or of life.

To me, the statue didn't just represent my mother, it also symbolized my family and everyone who missed me while I was away. Some people called her *La Loca*, "the madwoman", with her tangled hair and weary body. They said she had lost her sense of direction, literally and figuratively. But to me, she was perfectly sane. There was even a song by Maná, *El muelle de San Blas*, that felt like a tribute to her. It told the story of a woman who spent her whole life waiting at the harbor for her beloved, a man who left one day by boat and never came back.

That part of the promenade was farther from the city center and much quieter. It felt peaceful. The statue stood in a plaza surrounded by a low wall. It was the perfect spot to sit and talk.

"Want to sit on that wall, facing the sea?" I asked.

"Yeah, sounds great," he said with a smile.

We leaned our bikes next to us and sat on the wall, with the *Madre del Emigrante* behind us. The air was calm, and there was a light breeze. We spent a couple of hours catching up. I told him about Baltimore, my independence, life in the U.S., my plans… He told me about Gijón, his van, his projects. Daniel was in a good place, it showed. Things were going well for him, and little by little, he was finding his path. He wanted to travel with his diving work and lose himself in the crystal-clear waters of the world. He was still a free spirit.

Before we knew it, our conversation drifted toward memories of the past, and nostalgia settled in around us. We had slowly moved closer, and now our arms were touching. That afternoon, we didn't need any wine for old feelings to resurface, and for us to kiss. The first kiss was a soft one on the lips, followed by a long embrace that lasted several minutes. We had gone back to old patterns, but it felt natural. We couldn't help it.

"I've missed you so much all this time," he whispered in my ear as we stayed wrapped in each other's arms. "I don't know what I'm going to do with you. I know your life is somewhere else, but I have a weakness for you I just can't shake."

"Daniel… I've missed you too, your energy, your presence. You always make me smile when I think of you." I hugged him a little tighter.

"I'm so glad I ran into you at the Cuesta del Cholo the other day," he said, laughing.

"Right? What a beautiful coincidence. Maybe we were meant to find each other again."

"Yeah, maybe we're meant to be together…" He looked me in the eyes.

"I don't know what to say. Things have unfolded in such a strange way…"

"Yeah, that's true. But whatever happens, you can always text me. And when you're back in town… It would've been such a shame not to have seen you."

My feelings were all over the place at that point, and I didn't know what to say. Just a couple of months earlier, I had been obsessed with Yazid. I thought I still was, that I only had eyes for him. But now, with Daniel, those feelings were fading, and Yazid had been pushed into the background. With Daniel, it was easy to go from friendship to something romantic. He always seemed to be there for me, no matter how much time had passed or what had happened between us. He remained endlessly patient and tolerant, willing to be with me again and forget the past.

Sometimes I wished I could fall in love with him and forget Yazid for good. But why couldn't I? Something just didn't click, and I couldn't explain it. Maybe it was something chemical, irrational, or maybe it was something simpler, like the lack of stability I felt with him.

We stayed there, watching the sunset until nightfall. We both wanted to keep enjoying each other's company, so we decided to roll the afternoon into the evening and go out for dinner. We rode our bikes back to the Cimadevilla neighborhood and headed up to Lavaderu Square, the most iconic spot in the area and home to our favorite cider house. Aside from the croquettes, the food wasn't anything special, but it was the first restaurant we had ever gone to together, and it was full of good memories. We sat at a table on the terrace, side by side, talking about everything and nothing. As the night went on and the mood grew warmer, Daniel made me a proposal:

"Hey, I was thinking... would you like to sleep over at my place tonight?" he asked while squeezing my thigh under the table and smiling at me.

"If you insist..." I teased. "Of course I do. I've been waiting for you to ask me all through dinner." I leaned in and kissed him on the neck. I didn't care that people were around.

We rode our bikes to his place. Returning to that cobblestone street lined with old buildings and narrow balconies brought me right back to the past. He opened the old wooden door and we parked our bikes in the small entrance hall. I still remembered the green, geometric-patterned tile walls. We climbed the stairs to the fifth and top floor. He invited me in.

He'd done a great job redecorating, it looked much nicer than the last time I'd seen it. After showing me the living room, he took my hand and led me down the hall to his bedroom. His surfboard was propped up by the door, and his wetsuit hung on a hook across from it. The room had a bohemian yet elegant vibe, decorated in neutral colors. A hammock hung from the ceiling beams, right next to the bed. There were plants, and a desk sat beneath a slanted attic window.

He kissed me, one of those long, passionate kisses, as we tumbled onto the bed. He caressed my neck and moved down to my shoulders. We undressed and got lost beneath the sheets. That night, Daniel gave me the affection and tenderness I so badly needed. He was a balm, and he always would be.

We'd left the window open, and the morning light along with the sound of seagulls woke me up. Daniel, used to it, slept soundly. We were both naked, covered only by a white sheet. I felt a little cold and snuggled closer to him. It was a while before he woke up, but when he did, still half-asleep, he pulled me into his arms and kissed my shoulder, tickling me with his beard.

We lingered in bed until our stomachs started growling, and then decided to get dressed and head out for breakfast. Daniel loved the almond croissants from La Fe pastry shop, so we walked over to get a few. Their pastries were famous throughout the city, and those croissants usually sold out before lunchtime. We bought some to-go and walked to the marina. It was a perfect morning. We sat on a bench to eat and enjoy the morning sun. Daniel seemed lost in thought.

"Daniel, what are you thinking about? You're so quiet," I asked, pinching his cheek.

"Look," he began, "I know maybe this doesn't make much sense... but I want you to know that I still love you. And even though it's been a while, I haven't been able to forget you."

"Daniel…"

"Wait, let me finish," he interrupted. "Sometimes I think it has to mean something that, even after all these months apart, we still have this connection. The attraction, the affection are all still there, untouched. I want you to know that you'll always have a special place in my heart and in my mind. I'm not asking you to be my girlfriend. I know long distance is hard and that you have your own stuff and doubts, but I want you to know how I feel."

"I don't know what to say… I care about you so much, and you mean a lot to me. You're always there for me, despite everything that's happened. You've shown me so much over the years. Sometimes I feel like I don't even deserve how good you are to me."

"You don't have to think that way... Selfishly, I also do it for myself; I love spending time with you."

"Yeah, but... are we going to be like this forever? Together, on and off, every time we run into each other again?"

"I don't see anything wrong with that. We're both free." He pulled me closer and kissed me.

And that was where we left it.

The rest of the days were full of joy. I spent time with my family, with my friends, and with Daniel too. He never asked anything of me and always gave me space to make my own plans. No one was surprised to see us back together again. At that point, it was hard to explain what we had, let alone define it. But we both knew that, despite everything, there was still a unique and special bond between us that time and circumstance hadn't managed to break.

23

August 21, 2017

Baltimore, Maryland, United States

I arrived in Baltimore on a gray Sunday afternoon, under a heavy atmosphere. The city was empty, and there wasn't a soul on the streets. The air was hot and humid. I greeted the building's doorman, who welcomed me with a smile.

When I opened the door to my apartment, I was surrounded by silence, and for a moment I wished I were in Gijón. I had gotten used to my family's company, and the quiet felt unsettling. I left my suitcase in a corner, postponing the task of unpacking until the next day, and took a deep breath. I had just arrived and was already fantasizing about my next trip to Spain. I was exhausted and felt foolish. I collapsed onto the couch and turned on the TV to silence my thoughts.

To escape the end-of-summer nostalgia and the life in Gijón I had left behind, and now idealized, I threw myself into work and into completing my application for a Neurology residency spot. I didn't have much time; applications opened on September fifteenth.I sent my application to one hundred hospitals. It may have seemed like a lot, but the process was extremely competitive, and I had no idea how many interviews I would land. There were far more applicants than available residency spots, and although I had a strong resume, nothing was guaranteed.

After a couple of uncertain weeks, I finally started receiving interview invitations. I was thrilled, each invitation felt like a small victory. After all, every one of them represented a new opportunity to secure a residency and get closer to my goal of becoming a neurologist in the United States. Most came from hospitals in large cities like New York, Miami, or Chicago, but also from smaller places like Worcester or Cleveland. Each location offered its own climate and lifestyle, factors I also needed to consider.

Thankfully, the interviews were in-person, so I'd have the chance to experience those places and see which ones felt right. A few months of airports and packing and unpacking awaited me. It was a very important time in my professional life, and I was ready to enjoy it. My boss, who had supported many students through the same process in the past, encouraged me to accept all the invitations and turned a blind eye to my absences from work.

The first interview was in Philadelphia. I arrived in the city on the last train of the day and went straight to the hotel. I was nervous and couldn't think about anything but the next day's interview. I played out a thousand scenarios in my head, and the anxiety kept building. I hoped the people would be kind and that the doctors interviewing me wouldn't ask me anything too difficult. My mind felt foggy, and I didn't feel like doing anything, not even eating dinner.

I took a hot shower to relax and changed into pajamas. Before going to bed, I made myself iron my brand-new suit and hung it on the door. I ignored the television and turned off the light. "Tomorrow will be a good day," I told myself before closing my eyes. I tossed and turned for a while before finally falling asleep.

The next morning, I was awakened by the alarm on my phone, which I'd left next to my pillow. It took me a couple of minutes to remember where I was and why. Without letting myself linger, I got out of bed and put on my uniform: a black pantsuit paired with a white shirt. The mirror reflected an impersonal image. I was aiming for a professional look, but beneath those clothes, my personality disappeared. I tied my hair back in a braid and applied discreet makeup before heading to the hospital.

With a hint of timidity, I entered through the main door and walked up to the front desk. Before I could say anything, the receptionist pointed toward a group of people standing in a corner, also dressed in suits. I guess I looked the part.

I walked toward them with a steady step, trying to stay calm. They had formed a circle around a woman, all listening intently to what she was saying. She was petite but radiated confidence.

It was Betty, the program coordinator, and she was welcoming us while doing a headcount. She spoke fast and moved around constantly. Her face was deeply lined, and her hair was pulled back in a lacquered ponytail streaked with gray. It seemed like she had gone overboard with her makeup that morning, the pink eyeshadow made her look even older.

I put on my best smile and introduced myself. The situation felt unnatural. We were all wrapped in stiff, conservative suits, trying not to stand out. We hid our fears and insecurities behind forced smiles. No one knew what to say, and after the introductions, an awkward silence fell over the group. Thankfully, we didn't stay there long. Betty soon led us to a conference room.

It was a stuffy, windowless room that smelled like worn-out carpet, with a round table and chairs around it. She handed each of us a sheet with the day's full schedule. She also gave us a name tag with our name, where we were from, and the university we had attended. It felt like being labeled with a pedigree, a way to make quick judgments. Who we really were, our essence, faded into the background.

From eight in the morning onward, a series of formalities and unwritten codes of conduct shaped every interaction, with both the other applicants and anyone else we encountered. Every gesture and movement seemed rehearsed down to the smallest detail. Everyone was performing. Was I performing too?

I completed the five scheduled interviews, and as expected, the questions were exactly the same as the ones I'd read about in online forums. It became clear how scripted those interactions were, not designed to get to know the person behind the application, but simply to verify the résumé.

Finally, the day came to an end. Although all the conversations had gone well, I couldn't tell whether they liked me or not. Americans were very diplomatic, and you could never quite guess what lay behind their smiles. Still, I had completed my first interview without making any mistakes, and I felt satisfied. Even if it had all felt like choreography, I had danced it well. I tried to convince myself that this artificial feeling was just a matter of protocol, something I'd get used to with time, and I did.

With all the constant travel, I never had time to fully unpack my suitcase, and I got used to living out of it. Spending my days flying across the country became the new normal. I learned to enjoy waiting at the boarding gates and to tolerate the rush. I noticed how relative time became when my breakfast overlapped with travelers from other time zones drinking beer or eating dinner at nine in the morning. I stopped feeling self-conscious about dining alone and, whenever I could, I used the afternoons before each interview to explore the cities I was visiting.

One of my favorite places was the University of Chicago. I was influenced partly by my fond memories with Yazid, but also by Sofía, the Chilean girl I had met in Jordan. When we met, she was a med student in Chicago, and now she was a resident in Internal Medicine at one of the city's hospitals. We had stayed in touch off and on, and to help me save on hotel costs, she offered to host me at her place. I was really happy to see her again.

The afternoon I arrived, we went out for beers with some of her colleagues from the hospital, and she introduced me to several Neurology residents, including her boyfriend, Mike. Sofía was thriving in that city. She had a wide social circle and loved where she was doing her residency. She was an open book and shared the details of her life and her future plans. Even though she liked Chicago, she dreamed of returning to San Diego someday. She also confided in me how in love she was with Mike and her hopes of marrying him. I felt guilty for keeping quiet about Yazid, and for never having told her about my trips to Chicago. I regretted not being honest, but it was too late now. After all, Yazid was no longer part of my life.

I thought Chicago would be the perfect place to do my residency, until I discovered Dallas. It had slipped under the radar among better-known cities, but once I interviewed there, my perspective changed completely. Everyone was so warm and welcoming. Unlike the other interviews, they asked more personal questions and made me feel truly seen.

The program was comprehensive, and the residents rotated through three different hospitals: a community hospital for uninsured and low-income patients, a university/private hospital, and a veterans' hospital for soldiers, which in the U.S. operates as a separate network. It was clearly a unique opportunity to train as a neurologist. On top of that, the hospital had a group of doctors who specialized in multiple sclerosis, so

I'd be able to continue my research. I felt like I belonged there. I began dreaming of securing a spot in that program.

During the quieter moments of all that travel, I often thought about Yazid and how we had ended. I imagined what things would be like if he were also interviewing for residency spots, and how much closer we'd be to fulfilling our dream of being together. I felt a wave of frustration thinking, once again, about his sudden change of plans and how our paths had diverged. I tried to convince myself that things had happened the way they did for a reason, and that it had been for the best, but that thought only lasted a few minutes.

Sometimes I spiraled into negative thoughts and would feel sad. My sister had always been the rational voice in my head, and one day, during a phone call, she said something that helped me begin to heal from the wound Yazid had left behind.

"Lola, I understand that your feelings for Yazid are still mixed," Sara said in her usual calm voice.

"Well, tell me…"

"Sometimes people come into our lives to redirect our path, our trajectory." She paused before continuing. "For example, instead of thinking of Yazid as a mistake or someone who didn't keep his word, I'd think of him as someone who entered your life to guide you toward the path that led you to the U.S. to train as a neurologist."

"Yeah, but I don't know, Sara… Besides all that, I can't get out of my head all the things he said and never followed through on."

"What things? Why don't you focus on the good? You're growing so much over there, and he's been the driving force behind that."

Sara was right. My thoughts about Yazid were negative and served no real purpose. Yes, he had brought pain into my life, but there were many other things I could thank him for. Even though I'd made it this far through my own effort and hard work, I had to admit, he had been the main motivation for starting my career in the U.S.

If everything went well, I'd soon begin my neurology residency. It was time to look forward and let go of the past.

After a long wait, on March sixteenth, I received my acceptance letter for the residency program in Dallas. It was one of the happiest days I'd had in a long time.

Finally, after all that effort, I was going to be a neurologist! And in the place I had liked the most... Joy and fear wrapped around me in equal measure.

24

I had made it. After countless hours of studying, endless exams, and two years of research at Johns Hopkins, I was finally about to begin my Neurology residency. It took me several days to fully take it in. I couldn't stop smiling every time I shared the news with my family and friends. Everyone was genuinely happy for me, including my parents, who, even though they didn't like me being so far away, understood how important it was to me and supported me wholeheartedly.

March had been a month of milestones. One of my research projects had been accepted for presentation at the annual conference of the American Academy of Neurology. I would present it in May, in front of two hundred people. My work had received national recognition, proving to my supervisor that hiring me had been the right choice. That conference felt like the perfect way to close my chapter in Baltimore, with a flourish. More importantly, the results of my study were highly relevant to the treatment of multiple sclerosis. Presenting them there would be a major opportunity to raise awareness. The study revealed that African American patients experienced a much more aggressive form of multiple sclerosis than white patients. This was a key finding, as it could help inform better, more personalized treatment strategies for African American patients, and bring visibility to a population often overlooked by the scientific community.

After the excitement of the acceptance came a wave of insecurity and fear of not measuring up. I had never been good at public speaking, especially not in English, and definitely not in front of a crowd. I tended to talk too fast, and when I got nervous, it got even worse. I'd stumble over words and lose clarity. I had always dreaded giving presentations, whether in high school or college. I would speed through them as if the world were ending. But this time, I wasn't going to let that happen. I practiced my talk dozens of times, in front of the mirror, with friends, with anyone who would listen. My goal was to know it so well that when the time came, the words would flow naturally, and I could focus solely on keeping my pace.

Then came the week of my trip to Los Angeles, where the conference was taking place. I had seen the city hundreds of times in movies and on TV, and I had always dreamed of visiting. Neuroimmunology and L.A., a perfect combination. The convention would last about five days and be packed with talks and presentations. Technically, I wouldn't have much time to explore the city, but I was already planning to skip a few sessions for sightseeing. Luckily, my presentation was scheduled for the very first day. Once it was over, I'd be free to relax and enjoy both the symposium and the city.

I landed on a Monday night. After picking up a salad from a food stand at the airport, I went straight to the hotel to practice one last time. I was nervous. Every time I pictured myself speaking in front of that audience, my heart would pound. I needed to calm down and believe in myself. I practiced until one in the morning, and despite the time difference, it was already 4 a.m. back in Baltimore, I struggled to fall asleep.

The next morning, I woke up with puffy eyes and a foggy mind from the lack of sleep. I washed my face with cold water and tried to hide my fatigue behind good makeup. I reused the same suit I had worn for residency interviews and walked to the convention center, which was about ten minutes away. For a May morning, it was surprisingly cool, but I welcomed the cold air, it helped wake me up. The streets were nearly empty, and I passed only a few homeless people and some other attendees, easily identified by their formal outfits and name badges hanging from their necks.

When I arrived at the convention center, I went straight to the information desk, where they handed me a brochure with everything I needed to navigate the event. It included the full schedule, session titles, and a map of the venue. The conference was massive. At almost every time slot, five sessions were happening simultaneously. The amount of information was overwhelming, but it made me happy to see how many people were involved in neurology research. I was eager to hear about their progress and discoveries.

After reviewing the program and finding the room where I'd be presenting, I grabbed a coffee and made my way there. As I stepped inside, a chill ran down my spine and my heart began to race. The room seated at least four hundred people. I was thankful it was still only eight in the morning and that I had a couple of hours before my turn. I needed time to mentally prepare and calm my nerves. I decided to stay and watch the earlier presentations to get a feel for the setup, see how other speakers presented, and draw inspiration. I paid close attention to how they handled questions and began visualizing myself up there. If they could do it, I could too.

The session before mine wrapped up, and the moderator announced a fifteen-minute break. I took a deep, steady breath to settle my nerves. My session included four presentations of about twenty minutes each, and mine would be the second. I moved to the front row and sat beside the session moderator. I took the same seat that one of the earlier speakers had just vacated. A few minutes later, the other three presenters arrived. I greeted them shyly.

They were all men, around fifty, with an intellectual air. I was the only woman and by far the youngest, I didn't quite fit in. Two of them were American, and the third was Canadian. They all spoke polished, flawless English. We sat silently, facing forward, anxiously waiting for the session to begin. After a few minutes, the Canadian broke the silence:

"I don't know about you guys, but this is my first time presenting in front of so many people. I'm really nervous." His conference badge was pinned to his blazer. His name was Tom.

"Same here. Let's just hope the audience doesn't ask too many tough questions," I replied, relieved to know I wasn't the only one feeling that way.

"Don't worry, everything's going to be fine," said Peter, one of the Americans. From his tone and body language, he seemed like someone who'd been through it all. "Just remember, most of the time, the speaker knows more about the subject than anyone else in the room. And if you don't know the answer to a question, you can always say you'll look into it and follow up after the session."

"Well, yeah… when you put it that way," I replied, a little more at ease, though still not completely convinced.

After the fifteen-minute break, the moderator stepped onto the stage and officially opened our session. My heart started pounding again and rose to my throat. A tingling sensation crept up my hands. My mouth went dry. I took a deep breath from my diaphragm in a desperate attempt to steady my nerves. I had worked so hard, I couldn't afford to lose control.

The Canadian wrapped up his talk, and the applause marked the start of mine. The moderator called my name, and I walked up to the podium. My turn had come. I smiled at the audience and glanced quickly around the room, it was about half full. In the fourth row, my boss smiled back at me. He gave a little wave and winked. His presence calmed me.

As soon as I began speaking, the nerves and insecurities vanished. Without stumbling or stuttering, I delivered my presentation. The audience's questions weren't too difficult, and I was able to answer them confidently, which helped solidify my talk. When I finished, the applause, and later, my boss's congratulations, convinced me that I had done a good job.

After such a stressful morning, I was finally able to relax and enjoy the conference, where each talk was more interesting than the last. By around six in the evening, I headed out to explore the city. Since I didn't have much free time, I prioritized visiting Venice Beach, one of the most charming areas of Los Angeles. It was named after its many canals, reminiscent of Venice, lined with single-family homes, small gardens, and private docks that opened onto the water. Just ten minutes from the neighborhood was the beach itself. It seemed endless, with a boardwalk that stretched for miles and connected to Santa Monica, another one of the city's most famous districts.

I wandered the canal-lined streets and walked along the beach at sunset. The wind rustled the palm trees. People biked and skated along the boardwalk in short sleeves. I felt calm and proud of myself. My time in the U.S. was going well. For a moment, I imagined living there, and thought maybe the American dream felt a little like this.

The rest of my days in Los Angeles passed peacefully, walking from the hotel to the conference and enjoying the city. Even though it was huge and full of places to explore, I let them go. Every evening I could, I escaped to Venice Beach to watch the sunset, get lost in the canals, and stroll the shoreline.

On the last day of the convention, awards were given for the best presentations. To my surprise, my project won Best in the Young Investigators category. Receiving that award was a huge honor and the perfect final chapter to my time at Johns Hopkins. I returned to Baltimore with my head held high.

The final days in Baltimore, before leaving for Dallas were busy. I spent them tying up all my loose ends. I got rid of almost all my belongings, sold my furniture however I could, and closed the door to my downtown-view apartment for the last time.

I was sad to leave my coworkers behind, and especially my friends, Afsaneh and Amaya. I was going to miss my life in Baltimore, but who knew? Maybe one day I'd return to that city.

Looking back, I realized just how much I had grown over those two years. And most importantly, I had achieved my goal. Now, a new chapter was beginning, an exciting one: learning the art of Neurology and becoming the best doctor I could be.

221

25

June 23, 2018

Dallas, Texas, United States

I opened the door to my new apartment. It still smelled like paint and was completely empty. "Starting over again," I thought. I scanned the white walls, blank and void of personality. I imagined how I might decorate the space and mentally listed everything I'd need to furnish it. It was going to take a lot of energy to turn that empty place into a home. At that moment, everything felt like an uphill battle. I missed the comfort of Gijón and my family. I was exhausted. I leaned against the wall and slowly slid down to sit on the floor. All I could think about was sleeping, but I didn't even have a chair. I needed to go out and buy an air mattress and a set of sheets just to make it through the first night. Drained, I rested my head against the wall and closed my eyes for five minutes.

Those first few days were overwhelming. I spent them running back and forth between different stores, buying furniture and everything else for the apartment. There were also visits to the hospital to complete and sign the bureaucratic paperwork I needed before starting residency. And as if that weren't enough, I had to buy a car. In that city, having one was essential. Public transportation was neither reliable nor safe, and there were tons of places you could only get to by driving. With no time to think and out of pure necessity, I ended up buying a black 2008 Nissan Altima, its paint faded from the Texas sun. It was old and ugly, but at least it got the job done.

Somehow, amidst all that stress, my first week in Dallas passed, and oddly enough, I found myself missing my life in Baltimore. It was far from Spain or Europe, but at least I could live without a car and the lifestyle felt a little more European. I tried to focus on the present and what I had instead of comparing everything to what I no longer had. Was I always going to be this way? The same thing had happened with Gijón. I had a bad habit of only appreciating things after they were gone or had changed.

Among all the paperwork at the university, I also attended orientation meetings. That summer, sixty-eight of us were starting in Internal Medicine, and ten of us were Neurology residents. Even though they were separate programs, our first year in Neurology was entirely spent rotating through Internal Medicine, which is why we were grouped together.

The first meeting was a presentation in an auditorium, followed by a welcome reception. I felt shy, not knowing anyone. I've always seen myself as outgoing and social, but when it came to large groups like that, I struggled to break the ice and wasn't quite sure who to talk to or what to say.

To avoid awkward silences, I arrived just a minute before the presentation began and sat in one of the back rows next to a blond guy who was glued to his phone and didn't even flinch when I sat down. The room was full of new faces, and the whole situation was a bit overwhelming. During the talk, the department chair and other attending physicians welcomed us and wished us luck. I still couldn't quite believe that in less than a week, I'd be putting on a resident's coat and making medical decisions. The responsibility was daunting. I hoped the senior residents would guide us through the process and that the first days wouldn't be too rough. After having spent so much time focused on research, I felt like I had forgotten everything I once learned in med school.

After the presentation, we headed to the welcome reception in the university cafeteria. On the way there, small groups began to form. Many of the residents chatted and laughed easily, like they already knew each other. I felt a bit lost and didn't know who to talk to, so I went straight for the cocktail table, hoping someone would strike up a conversation along the way.

While I was waiting for the bartender, a girl came up and started talking to me. I sighed in relief. Her name was Tanya, and she was also starting her Neurology residency. She smiled nonstop and talked really fast. She invited me to join a group of residents. They were all American, most from Texas. Interestingly, nearly all of them wore engagement rings, and a few already had kids and were proudly showing off pictures of their families. I knew the southern U.S. was conservative, but I hadn't expected it to be quite so traditional. I was surprised. We were all roughly the same age, but living in completely different life stages. Between that and my accent, I felt out of place, like an outsider. For a moment, I wondered if I had chosen the wrong place. But I made an effort to shift my mindset. I barely knew them, I didn't want to judge too quickly. Their relationship status didn't have to affect our ability to connect. After all, our goal was the same: to become fully trained physicians.

With no time to rest, June 30 arrived. It was the last afternoon before residency began, and I panicked. The insecurity returned and took over me. I started to worry I wouldn't measure up to my peers. In search of reassurance, I reached out to Sofía, who was already a second-year resident and had been through all of it. I sent her a message, and we ended up talking on the phone for a couple of hours. She calmed me down and gave me advice on how to survive the first days.

"I totally get your nerves, it's normal," she said in a soothing voice.

"And I won't lie to you. It's not going to be easy. You're going to feel like you don't know anything more than once. But don't forget: if you've made it this far, you're capable of anything."

"Thanks, darling. I'll try to think that way, but I feel like I don't even know how to take a medical history or assess a patient anymore."

"That's the least of it. After a couple of times, you'll see how naturally it all starts to flow. I'll send you an email with tips for patient histories. If you follow this system, you won't have any trouble," she continued, trying to reassure me. "It's all very systematic."

"Thank you so much, really." Her words were incredibly comforting.

"You're very welcome! Besides, you'll always have senior residents around to guide you through the process. Everything's going to be great!"

We kept talking about residency for quite a while, and then the conversation shifted to other things, unrelated to medicine. We caught up on everything that had happened since the last time we'd seen each other in Chicago. Sofía had saved a surprise for the end.

"Lola, by the way, I have to tell you something. Not many people know yet, but... it's official!"

"What's official?" I asked, full of curiosity.

"I'm getting married! Mike proposed last weekend."

"Congratulations! Why didn't you tell me sooner? And here we are, talking about nonsense... I'm so happy for you!"

"Thanks, love!" She was glowing with joy. "We're planning to get married in San Diego next May. I know it'll be tough with your residency schedule, but I'd love for you to come. Even with the distance, I consider you a good friend and care about you a lot."

"Of course! I'd love to be there to celebrate such a special day with you and your family. If my schedule allows, I'll be there."

After we hung up, I found myself wondering who else she'd invite to the wedding and whether I'd know anyone there. The possibility of Yazid being one of the guests crossed my mind, but I quickly dismissed it. He was most likely working somewhere in the Middle East and wouldn't have time for something like that. Not that it mattered. He was no longer part of my life, and we hadn't spoken in over a year. We'd chosen different paths, and even though it wasn't the one we had once dreamed of, it was the reality now. I pushed the thought from my mind, got everything ready for the next day, and went to bed.

I'd be lying if I said the beginning of residency was easy. Every day felt like a challenge, and every patient was a puzzle. Though I never acted on it, there were many days when I fantasized about running away, pretending none of it had ever happened. The American healthcare system was completely different from Spain's, and I felt like I was learning to be both a medical student and a resident all over again. On top of that, my two years in research had distanced me from clinical work and patient care, which made everything more difficult. I had forgotten more than I realized.

A typical day at the hospital started around six in the morning. Each first-year resident was assigned a list of patients. As soon as we arrived, we had to check their vital signs and lab results, examine them, and create a treatment plan. Everything had to be ready by nine, when the attending physician would arrive. Then we would go over the information and the plan together, before doing patient rounds as a team.

For me, the hardest part was presenting the case in an organized way during rounds. I would get nervous, skip important details, or lose my train of thought. Thankfully, we often had medical students rotating with us, and as part of their training, they presented one or two patients themselves. That meant I didn't always have to present, which made my mornings much easier. I listened carefully to their presentations and tried to mimic their tone and structure.

The first six months of residency felt like a nonstop sprint to learn how the system worked and how to practice medicine within it. Our rotations took place across three different hospitals. At first, I thought it was great to be exposed to a variety of settings, but over time, I began to see it as a disadvantage. Just as I was getting used to the workflow and getting to know the nurses in one hospital, it would be time to move to another.

I worked in a wide range of specialties: Internal Medicine, ICU, Cardiology, Nephrology... The learning curve was steep, but I barely had any free time and felt completely drained. Every day felt the same, and I lost track of what a weekend was supposed to be. There were Saturdays and Sundays when I wouldn't leave the hospital until 7 p.m. The only clue that it wasn't a weekday was when I passed the pool at my apartment complex, full of people drinking and having fun. I felt like life was passing me by, and with each month, I grew more exhausted.

I dreamed of taking a vacation, and my first break came in February. It was an odd month for time off, but I hadn't been able to choose the dates. I only had seven days in the middle of winter. If I went to Gijón, I'd waste too much time traveling.

Plus, with the cold and rainy weather, everyone would be busy with their routines. I wouldn't be able to enjoy my time there. I needed to find a better option.

After thinking it over for several days, I decided not to go to Spain and instead travel somewhere in Latin America. It had been on my to-do list, and this felt like the perfect moment. I read through several travel forums and finally chose Costa Rica: it was nearby, a natural paradise, and considered one of the safest countries in Central America. None of my friends could come with me, but I didn't mind the idea of traveling alone. After all, my life in the U.S. had been a solo journey from the beginning.

I didn't overthink it, I just booked a flight to San José. My final destination would be Puerto Viejo, a coastal town in the south of the country, where the crystal-clear waters of the Caribbean Sea awaited me.

26

February 26, 2019

San José, Costa Rica

We landed around eleven in the morning. As soon as the plane came to a stop, the aisle filled with restless travelers. Impatient, they opened the overhead bins and grabbed their luggage. They were eager to get going and enjoy the country, there was no time to waste. The flight attendant opened the cabin door, and the passengers hurried off. I was seated near the back, so I was one of the last to leave. Instead of a jet bridge connecting to the terminal, I was met with a narrow metal staircase leading directly to the tarmac.

The moment I stepped outside, a wave of humid heat hit me in the face. The air was heavy and overwhelming, and it was hard to move forward. Rays of sunlight filtered through the clouds and reflected off puddles scattered across the runway. It looked like it had just stopped raining. The air smelled of wet earth.

I followed the arrows painted on the ground until I reached the terminal and let out a sigh of relief as the cool air conditioning hit my face. It was going to take some getting used to, that kind of heat. At the entrance was a huge sign that read *Pura Vida*. It was a signature expression of Costa Rica, and it meant several things. It could be used as a greeting, or to answer "very well" when someone asked how you were doing. But its meaning went far deeper—it embodied the Costa Rican or "Tico" philosophy of life. In those two words, *Pura Vida*, came together the ideas of complete well-being, the art of living well, and an embrace of the simple and natural. I thought it was a wise expression, one that reflected a mindset completely opposed to American capitalist culture.

Many new arrivals stopped to take a photo in front of the sign, but all I could think about was getting to Puerto Viejo, so I kept walking. After going through customs, I exited the terminal to find the minibus I had reserved to take me to my final destination. I had imagined the transportation area would be organized, with signs and clear directions. Instead, I found chaos: tourists tangled up with their luggage and relentless taxi drivers offering rides to anyone who crossed their path. As if that weren't enough, the drivers for the various private shuttle companies were yelling out the names of passengers who still hadn't identified themselves.

It was impossible to understand anything. I had to circle the area several times, pushing through with my backpack, before I finally spotted the driver. He was wearing a blue vest with Viajes Paraíso printed on the back, the company I had booked with. Relieved, I hurried over to him, and ten minutes later we were on the road.

The drive to Puerto Viejo was longer than expected, it lasted about seven hours and felt endless. There was no highway, and we had to stop frequently because of road construction and slow-moving trucks. We passed through modest towns and palm forests. Rain and sun alternated several times until night fell. Just as I felt sleep weighing down my eyelids, the driver announced we were getting close and would start dropping people off at their hotels.

The road was narrow and surrounded by dense trees. There were no lights, and I could hardly see anything, only the silhouettes of branches. There was no sign of civilization. You'd think we were lost.

A few minutes later, we took a left turn and the landscape opened up. The bus was now driving along the coast. The nearly full moon reflected on the waves, revealing glimpses of the beauty around us. In the distance, I could see Puerto Viejo.

The minibus gradually emptied as we drove through the town and stopped along the way. It still had the charm of a small coastal village and looked fairly modest in size. There were hotels and restaurants with patios, but most of the buildings were simple and low-rise, no more than three stories tall. Many of the roads were unpaved. There were no sidewalks, and people walked along the edge of the road.

We left the urban area and were back on a dark road again. I started to worry that the driver had forgotten about me when the bus came to a stop. We had arrived. Finally. I got off quickly.

The hostel was called Selina, and it was across the road. I crossed carefully and entered through a wooden gate. There was a parking area with a few bikes and cars. I could hear the chirping of crickets. I followed a gravel path until I found the reception.

I was greeted by a girl with a sun-kissed glow and an Argentine accent. She was friendly and warm, and quickly started telling me her story. Her name was María, and she had come to Puerto Viejo intending to spend just one week on vacation. But she had fallen in love with the place and decided to make it her new home. She'd been living there for three years. For a moment, I envied the freedom and flexibility of her lifestyle.

We chatted about her time in Puerto Viejo, and she recommended several beaches and places to visit. She insisted I rent a bike to get around. She handed me a lanyard with the hostel keys and took me upstairs to my room. On the way, she showed me where the bathrooms were, they were shared, and where the bar was. Reggae music played, and the vibe was lively. I would've liked to have a drink, but I was exhausted. After a hot shower, I went straight to bed and was out within minutes.

I woke up naturally, without an alarm, to the morning light. It was hot, and the air felt heavy. The room was tiny and didn't have air conditioning. From bed, I stretched out to open the window, then lazily lay back down. I could hear birds chirping, and the soft clinking of breakfast dishes and chatter from the bar. Trying to put off getting up, I reached for my phone and got distracted checking messages, then lost myself scrolling through Facebook and other mindless pages.

By nine, the grumbling in my stomach reminded me I still hadn't eaten breakfast. I got out of bed and got dressed in the narrow space between the bed and the wall. I packed my beach bag with little more than a towel, sunscreen, and a book, then headed down to the front desk. María, the Argentine girl from the night before, was there. Her face looked fresh, and she smiled when she saw me.

"¡Good morning!" she said cheerfully.

"Pura vida!" I replied, trying to match her energy. "Do you still have bikes to rent?"

"Of course! It's five dollars for the day. Just make sure to bring it back before sunset for safety."

"No problem. Thanks! By the way... which beach did you recommend yesterday? I can't remember the name."

"Playa Uva. It's my favorite. About fifteen minutes by bike in the opposite direction of town. And if you haven't had breakfast yet, there's a little café in a tree about five minutes from here, on the way. It's super cool."

"You read my mind. Thanks again!"

"Anytime!"

I grabbed the bike and rode off with another smile. The ride itself was an experience. The road was perfectly flat and smooth, flanked by lush greenery. Palms and trees in a shade of green so vivid it looked unreal, their leaves shaped in ways I'd never seen before. There was barely any traffic, just cyclists who smiled as they passed by.

After breakfast and a coffee, I continued on toward Punta Uva. I followed the dreamlike road until I saw a sign for the beach. I took the unpaved path down to the shore. The sand was white, and the sea was a brilliant turquoise. A soft ocean breeze made it all the more perfect. Several bikes were locked to palm trees, and there were hardly any people around. I locked mine and, feeling hot from the ride, walked straight toward the water. The sand was burning beneath my feet. I dipped my toes in, the temperature was perfect, and then dove right in. I lost track of time, floating in those crystal-clear waters you only see on travel magazine covers.

The Caribbean sun was brutal, and I didn't realize how badly I was burning until I got out of the water. My skin was already turning red, which worried me. In Spain, I usually wouldn't feel a sunburn until the end of the day, so I knew this one was going to hurt. In the back of my mind, I heard my sister's voice saying, "You never put on enough sunscreen!" And it was true, I hadn't put on any. I'd forgotten how close we were to the equator and how much stronger the sun was here. I had learned the hard way. I needed to find shade as soon as possible. I had to head back.

Once I dried off a bit, I left the beach and made it back to the hostel around lunchtime. After stopping by my room to change, I went to the bar for some shade. I planned to order food and stay there all afternoon reading.

The bar was open-air, with Caribbean-style decor and a wooden floor. Ceiling fans stirred the air with a gentle breeze, and the laid-back music made it easy to linger. I was glad it was open all day. I settled into one of the armchairs. The waiter, a tall, dark-skinned guy, came over quickly.

"Pura vida! What can I get you?" he asked, flashing a perfect smile with full lips.

"Hi!" I smiled back. "Can I get a beer and a burger with fries?" He was very attractive. I felt nervous and wasn't even sure why.

"Coming right up!" He smiled again.

I noticed he held eye contact. I tried not to read too much into it, telling myself it was just cultural and he was probably just being polite. I'd been single for too long, and sometimes loneliness distorted my perception. I tended to see things that weren't really there.

Just five minutes later, he came back with the beer.

"By the way, I have a question," he said, locking eyes with me again. "I can't quite place your accent... Where are you from?"

"From Asturias, in northern Spain," I answered shyly, feeling my face heat up. I hoped I wasn't visibly blushing. "Are you from here?"

"The Princess of Asturias?" he joked. "I'm from San José, but I moved here a couple of years ago to work. Beautiful place, isn't it?"

"Yes, it's stunning, though it's a shame I got sunburned on my first day…" I pointed to my arms.

"Yeah, you're pretty red… The sun's strong here, especially if you're not used to it. Get some aloe vera and put it on your skin, they sell it at the pharmacy in town," he advised. "Anyway, I'm getting distracted! I'll be right back with your food."

Just like that, he turned and headed back to the bar. I watched him walk away, curious, and realizing how much I wanted to know more about him. I glanced over at him now and then as he worked. He really was attractive. He returned ten minutes later.

"Here's your burger. You picked the best thing on the menu."

"Thanks!" I said, grabbing a fry without hesitation.

"My pleasure." He started to turn away, then paused. "Actually, I was thinking…" He hesitated a moment, then looked at me again. "I get off at six. If you'd like, we could go for a bike ride. I could show you around."

"Sure!" I answered, trying not to sound too eager. "I'll be here reading. I need to hide from the sun, you know!"

"Perfect. By the way, I'm Matías. Nice to meet you."

"Nice to meet you! I'm Lola."

"Lola… Beautiful name. See you later!"

I picked up a few more fries as I replayed what had just happened and marveled at how spontaneous it all was. Part of me worried about the risk of going off with a total stranger. But the other part reassured me. There was nothing wrong with it, and he probably was just a normal guy.

That internal debate about whether it was a good idea or not lasted exactly as long as it took to devour the burger. What could really go wrong? The idea that something bad might happen felt like paranoia. I needed to let go a little in life. I was going to give this Matías guy a chance. After all, it was just a sunset bike ride...

27

I spent the rest of the afternoon at the hostel bar, reading and staying out of the sun. Every now and then, I'd look up from my book and glance over at Matías as he worked. His skin was dark, and he had a strong build. He wore a polo with the hostel logo stretched across his back and arms. The more I looked at him, the more I wanted to get to know him.

Sometimes he caught me staring, but instead of looking away, I held his gaze. He played along, answering with a wink. Maybe I was being a bit bold, but I was enjoying the flirtation. I wondered how many solo travelers he'd done this with before me. Honestly, I didn't care.

There was about half an hour left in his shift when he came over to my table.

"A piña colada for the Princess of Asturias. On the house," he said, setting it down. "See you at the front in thirty?"

"Thank you! You didn't have to…" I smiled, picking up the glass for a sip. "Okay. I'll see you at the entrance."

"Perfect." He smiled back.I finished the cocktail faster than usual. I was a little nervous and needed the alcohol to loosen up. I took the last sip, closed my book, and headed to my room to change.

We met by the bikes at the hostel entrance. The sun was low in the sky, and though it was still warm, the heat had eased. Travelers were coming and going—some arriving with backpacks, alone or in pairs. Matías smiled and motioned for me to follow him.

We headed in the opposite direction from town, and after a few minutes on that familiar road, Matías turned onto a narrow, unpaved path that was easy to miss. I felt a flicker of unease— we were moving away from populated areas, and if anything went wrong, I wouldn't be able to call for help. I pushed the thought away and kept following.

The path opened up to a small overlook with a view of the sunset over the ocean. The scene was stunning.

"Beautiful, isn't it?" he said with a smile. "I found this place by accident one day."

"I love it!" I leaned my bike against a tree and stepped closer to the edge. "Thanks for bringing me here."

Matías sat on a rock and gestured for me to join him. We stayed mostly silent, taking in the view. The quiet wasn't awkward. I felt at ease in his presence. There was no one else around. A few people stopped by, but as if sensing they were intruding, they didn't stay long.

We remained there until the sun had fully set. It was getting dark, and we needed to head back. I started to stand up, but

242

Matías took my hand and gently pulled me toward him to kiss me. It had been months since anyone had kissed me. His lips were full and soft. I melted into him.

"Lola, Lola, Lola…" he murmured. "I could stay here with you for hours, but it's getting dark, and riding back through that bumpy trail will be tough. Plus, you have to return your bike or María's going to come after you."

"You're right," I said, still catching my breath. Those kisses had stirred up a desire in me that had been dormant for far too long.

"Shall we?" He stood and offered his hand. "Want to come to my place tonight? I live five minutes from the hostel. I watched a Spanish movie the other day that cracked me up. I'd love to watch it again with you."

"Mmm, your place?" I gave him a sideways smile. "Honestly, you've left me wanting to spend more time with you." I kissed his neck, playing along.

"Me too! Come on, you'll have a great time, I promise."

We rode back to the hostel and exchanged numbers. He gave me his address, and we agreed to meet in a couple of hours. We said goodbye with a hug and a kiss on the cheek. I watched him ride off toward town.

From the very beginning, I knew that invitation meant more than just watching a movie, but I was the first one interested. It was the perfect chance to let go and enjoy myself. I was far from Dallas, and this little adventure wouldn't affect my life in any real way. It would be a travel romance—another experience. After all, I was a free, independent woman.

Before leaving the hostel, I messaged Amaya and Afsaneh to tell them where I was going. It probably wouldn't help much if something happened, but it made me feel safer. Still slightly wary, I got into the taxi.

Matías lived on a side street off the main road lined with restaurants. The road was unpaved, and the houses were modest, all in different shapes and colors. He was waiting for me on the steps of what looked like his house. When he saw me, he smiled and came to open the taxi door.

"I thought you weren't coming," he said, wrapping an arm around me and kissing me.

"Here I am, but don't think I didn't go back and forth about it a hundred times," I teased. "Everyone in Baltimore has your phone number and address. If anything happens, they know where to find you."

I said it jokingly… but I meant it, just a little.

"Beautiful, I get your concern, and it's good that you're cautious, but you don't need to worry with me. Come on…" He took my hand, gently urging me to follow.

We climbed the brown tiled stairs. His place was a small, simple studio. There was barely more than a bed and an old wooden wardrobe, worn from years of use. The only window was covered with a Bob Marley blanket acting as a curtain. There wasn't much else in the apartment. The kitchen, if you could call it that, was outside on the terrace and consisted of just a fridge and a sink.

What struck me was how naturally Matías carried himself, like he couldn't care less about appearances or how modest his place was. It seemed like his hostel job didn't pay much, although maybe he was saving everything he could to send money back to his family in the capital. In that moment, I realized how little we really knew about each other. How old was he? What were his hobbies? Did he have siblings? Kids? Maybe none of that mattered. Maybe it was better not to know. What mattered now was simply being present, in the moment, and enjoying our time together.

Matías stepped out onto the terrace and came back with a bottle of wine. We lay down on the bed, and he placed his laptop on his lap. The movie was called *Toc*. I'd never heard of it before, it didn't seem very well known, but it was funny.

We were close, but not touching. The tension between us was palpable. I was dying to kiss him, so I made the first move. I kissed him softly, and he kissed me back. He leaned over to set the laptop on the floor and pulled me toward him. The kisses quickly led to caresses. We began to undress each other. His muscular arms and chest looked even more attractive without a shirt. His eyes were a mesmerizing shade of green, I couldn't stop staring at them.

Matías was a god of pleasure. Even though he barely knew me, he instinctively knew how to find me, what to do, when, and how. It was uncanny, like he was a pro. Maybe he was the hostel's gigolo. Maybe what he was doing with me that night, he'd done with many others before. That would explain why he was so good at it, but I didn't care. In that moment, I didn't mind being "this week's traveler". In fact, I was glad he'd chosen me.

That night, I felt free and completely in control of my life. I was finally breaking free from the love triangle with Yazid and Daniel. With Matías, I realized there was an entire world still waiting to be discovered, and that I could meet someone when I least expected it.

We fell asleep and didn't wake up until the next morning. The birdsong stirred me, and it took me a few minutes to orient myself and remember everything that had happened the night before. I looked at him and could hardly believe how things had unfolded, but at the same time, I felt empowered. I was discovering a side of myself I hadn't known before. Letting go of my inhibitions had been cathartic.

I would've loved to stay in his arms all morning, but Matías had to go to work. In his tiny terrace kitchen, he made scrambled eggs and toast. We stood by the counter, eating breakfast while chatting about nothing in particular, birds chirping in the background.

He took me back to the hostel on his bike. He stood up to pedal while I sat on the seat, holding onto his waist. We wobbled and laughed like teenagers trying not to fall.

Matías brought out a carefree, spontaneous side of me, one I had long suppressed under the seriousness of my environment and my life in the U.S.

We said goodbye at the hostel entrance with a kiss. He went off to the bar, and I went back to my room. Before returning to the beach, I napped for a couple of hours. I hadn't slept well and was completely drained.

Puerto Viejo was surpassing all my expectations. From that night on, I didn't sleep alone again. Even though Matías had first come across as someone of few words, I soon learned he was incredibly social and loved to talk. I found out he had friends on nearly every corner of the town. They were a mix of locals and long-term travelers who were on their way to becoming locals themselves. Some had fascinating stories, though most were just escaping lives they'd grown unhappy with. Once they discovered this paradise, they couldn't resist. They left their old lives behind to start anew in this place. They had fallen in love with the sea, the simplicity of Puerto Viejo, and its *pura vida*. María at the front desk was the best example of that.

Those experiences gave me a different perspective. I realized that a "perfect life" didn't have to mean a structured one. Those standards were subjective, and most of the time, they came from external expectations rather than our own desires. I imagined what it would be like to live in that place permanently.

For a few moments, I was tempted to hop on that train and leave all of Dallas behind. Life there was simple. Material things barely mattered. Nature and human connection carried far more weight than work. In the end, everything is relative, and the environment we live in shapes our behavior more than we realize. That trip made me see how my essence had started to fade under the endless days in the hospital.

That week, I spent as much time with Matías as I could. I knew that once those days were over, our story would end too. So I made the most of it. When he wasn't working, we went to the beach or explored nearby places. At night, we always slept together, either at his place or mine.

It was impossible not to grow fond of him, but I never lost sight of reality. I made a conscious effort to keep our relationship from slipping from the physical into the emotional. This time, I knew, we came from completely different worlds. The healthiest, most realistic thing was not to create expectations or make plans. What we had would remain just that, an adventure. There would be no reunions. After everything I'd been through with Yazid, I'd learned that the romances and flings you experience while traveling are best left behind when the trip ends. No promises, no phone calls.

I returned to Dallas full of energy, and full of *pura vida*. It had been a liberating trip, one that helped me reclaim my confidence and see life from a new angle. It reminded me that there's a whole world of possibilities out there, just waiting for me.

28

I woke up in a hotel room in the La Jolla neighborhood, in a giant bed with soft white sheets. No alarm, after ten hours of sleep. It had been a long week, and I needed to recover. Luckily, it wasn't past nine and I still had a few hours—the wedding of Sofía and Mike wouldn't start until five. I wanted to make the most of it and explore, especially to see the ocean I missed so much.

Refusing to give in to laziness, I got up. When I opened the curtains, sunlight flooded the room. It was a perfect morning for a walk. I quickly threw on the first things I could find: the black leggings from the day before and a loose white t-shirt. With a freshly washed face and my hair pulled into a ponytail, I was ready.

Before leaving the hotel, following American custom, I grabbed a to-go coffee from the café in the lobby and headed toward the beach. The air was crisp and clean, and the temperature was just right. Palm trees lined the streets. There was barely any traffic, and everything felt calm.

On my way to the beach, I passed morning walkers, neighbors walking their dogs, and the occasional jogger. Everyone looked genuinely happy. I admired the dreamy homes along the way and imagined what it would be like to live in a place like this. For some reason, it reminded me a lot of Somió, a neighborhood in Gijón. Both had that exclusive feel, tucked away from the city center, nestled among rolling hills, with standalone houses surrounded by trees and luxury cars parked in their driveways.

The street led me straight to the oceanfront at La Jolla Beach. Perfectly aligned palm trees swayed in the sea breeze, and seagulls flew in circles overhead. I took off my sneakers and walked barefoot through the fine sand until I dipped my feet in the cold water. There were surfers catching waves and a few others farther out doing stand-up paddleboarding.

I walked along the shore until I reached the Memorial Pier, a long wooden structure stretching into the sea. At the far end, a few fishermen were casting lines, hoping for a bite. I sat on a bench nearby and curiously watched what they might catch. I stayed there a long while, but they didn't seem to have much luck—only pulling up tangled seaweed. Fishing clearly required patience, which I lacked. What I *did* have was hunger. I gave up on watching and made my way back in search of something to eat.

Just past the boardwalk, I found a small spot that served sandwiches, smoothies, and colorful juices. It looked like one of those trendy health cafés made popular by Hollywood celebrities, promoting detox diets. Hanging plants decorated the ceiling and walls. They championed eco-conscious living, and all the packaging, including the straws, was made from recycled materials. I sat at a table facing the street and devoured a chicken and cheese sandwich with tomato. I paired it with a green juice made from apple, cucumber, and spinach, but it tasted like grass. Without getting too distracted, I headed back to the hotel as soon as I finished eating. I still had three hours before the wedding, but I didn't want to be rushing. There'd be time to explore more tomorrow.

Getting ready for a wedding was a whole ritual, and mine started with a bubble bath. While the tub filled with water, I played Dua Lipa's latest album and took the dress out of its garment bag. I checked it for wrinkles and snipped off the price tag; it was brand new for tonight. It was long and flowy, a bold shade of red, halter-necked, with an open back and shoulders.

I'd always wanted a dress like that and couldn't wait to wear it. The bathroom was filled with steam and the scent of vanilla. I relaxed under the bubbles for half an hour, until my fingertips were all pruney. Wrapped in a white towel, I curled my hair and let it fall loosely over my shoulders. Thankfully, I nailed the eyeliner on the first try and didn't take long with my makeup. I was nearly ready. I slipped into the dress and paired it with long gold earrings and matching flat sandals. I smiled at my reflection, I liked what I saw.

The wedding was taking place at the d'Auberge hotel, located north of the city, on the outskirts of San Diego. From the photos, it looked like an idyllic place to get married. The ceremony would be held in the garden, overlooking the ocean, and both the cocktail hour and dinner would take place in the same spot. Sofía had been planning the wedding for months, and I knew everything would be perfect. A few days earlier, she had told me there would be about a hundred guests, a mix of family and friends. I had mentioned my concern about not knowing anyone, but she reassured me that I wouldn't feel left out for even a second. She'd said it with a mysterious tone I couldn't quite interpret. I chose to believe her and just go with the flow, no matter how awkward things might get.

The taxi dropped me off at the hotel entrance. As soon as I stepped inside, I entered a lobby with gleaming floors and luxurious, light-filled chandeliers. It was an open space with high ceilings. To the right, an archway led into one of the salons where a piano was playing. Elegance filled every corner. One of the front desk attendants led me to the garden where the wedding would take place.

The venue was even more beautiful than I had imagined. Every detail was perfect. The altar, facing the ocean, was framed by an arch of white flowers, matching the white ribbons that adorned the guests' chairs. Off to the side was a piano, where a man in a white tuxedo played a piece that reminded me of Debussy. He has been one of my father's favorite composers when I was a child. The sun was inching toward the water, and the light turned golden. It was a magical place to get married.

The bride and groom hadn't arrived yet, but several guests were already there, wine and champagne glasses in hand, chatting and greeting each other warmly. I recognized Sofía's brothers from photos and, a little shyly, introduced myself. They were just as friendly and smiling as she was. They greeted me kindly and introduced me to several family members and friends. I felt instantly welcome and had a good feeling about the evening. I also spotted some of Sofía's colleagues from the hospital and went over to say hello. After a brief chat, I took a stroll around the spectacular garden and headed to the bar for a glass of champagne.

While I waited for the bartender to serve me, a familiar voice said my name from behind. I turned around and nearly jumped—there was Yazid. It had been over two years since I'd last seen him. Facing him again after so long was a shock.

"Lola! What a surprise. How are you? Sofía didn't tell me you were coming," he said with a smile as he stepped in to hug me.

"Yazid! It's been so long," I said, trying to mask my surprise as my heart began to race. I hoped he didn't notice.

"I'm really glad to see you," he said as he hugged me.

"Same here. Honestly, I didn't expect to see you here. I thought you were in the Middle East?"

"Well, as you can see, I'm here. What about your boyfriend?" he asked, straight to the point.

"I came alone," I replied vaguely, knowing he'd have to push if he wanted a real answer. "And you? Where are your four wives?" I teased, genuinely curious.

"Lola, I don't have one, or two, or three." His expression turned serious for a moment. "I'm single. And you?" he asked again, though I knew he already had the answer.

"I'm single too. I've been focusing on other things," I said with a smile, glancing at his lips. It took less than five minutes for me to fall right back into his orbit.

That unexpected reunion hit like a head-on collision, and I could feel the energy between us. It had taken us both by surprise, and the sheer spontaneity of it revealed the tension still lingering beneath the surface. After a few direct exchanges, the mood softened, and the conversation shifted to catching up. Our lives had taken different paths.

Not much had changed for Yazid; he was still traveling constantly for his family's business. He was now a partner in the company and owned a stake in it. He was doing very well and didn't miss medicine one bit. Most weeks, he was somewhere in the Middle East, though he still made occasional trips to the U.S. for business deals. He'd scheduled meetings in San Francisco and L.A. to justify the long journey and attend the wedding. I told him about Dallas, about my neurology residency, my sleepless hospital nights... My life was mostly work these days. We talked about our families, about Amman, about Gijón... But we avoided the subject of our relationship. The last days we spent together were long gone and no longer worth rehashing. We were nothing more than old acquaintances now. And yet, despite the time and distance, the chemistry between us hadn't faded. I could have talked to him for hours.

Yazid wore a navy suit that hugged his frame, with a white shirt and a pale blue tie. He hadn't changed much, though the past two years had clearly taken their toll. Fine lines had begun to appear between his eyebrows and beneath his eyes. His hairline had receded a bit, and though it was hidden beneath his beard, his jaw looked sharper. He'd changed, but he was still as attractive as ever, maybe even more so.

I found myself staring at him, remembering the intimacy we once shared, and feeling a deep desire to relive it. All this time I had convinced myself Yazid was nothing more than a neutral figure in my mind. But I realized now that had been an illusion, I was still vulnerable to his presence. His voice gave me chills, and his scent transported me straight to the past. It was clear I hadn't truly forgotten him.

As we talked, the sea breeze tousled my hair, and at one point, Yazid gently brushed a strand from my lips, his hand lingering on my cheek. I looked at him, surprised, and he gave me that playful look I knew so well. It was amazing how quickly we could rewind time. The more we talked, the more the emotions began to resurface, a mix of longing and bitterness. I still held some resentment, but I couldn't deny the magnetic pull I felt toward him.

The groom finally arrived and began greeting guests, and everyone started to take their seats. Since neither of us knew many people, we decided to sit together during the ceremony. To an outsider, we looked just like any other couple.

Moments later, Sofía arrived in a shiny black vintage car. She looked stunning and radiated happiness. The pianist began to play the wedding march. Hand in hand with her father, she walked down a short aisle scattered with red rose petals. Up close, she was even more beautiful, wearing a white lace dress, her hair in a bun, and a veil cascading down her back. She smiled as she passed each row of guests, and when she saw Yazid and me sitting together, her smile grew even wider. For a second, I wondered if this whole reunion had been planned, but quickly dismissed the idea. She had never known the full story between us.

The ceremony was magical, and the couple said their vows just as the sun touched the sea. The rest of the evening was filled with emotion and heartfelt speeches from family and close friends. As if pulled by an invisible force, Yazid and I stayed by each other's side the entire time. We enjoyed the wedding, danced and laughed with the couple and other guests. There were moments of undeniable connection, when we joked about our shared past, or when we locked eyes while dancing to a romantic song. The tension kept building all night until neither of us could pretend anymore.

29

It was midnight, and the end of the wedding was starting to show. The dance floor had gradually emptied, and many of the guests had already left. It was time to say goodbye to the newlyweds, and to Yazid. I felt like the night had slipped away without me realizing it, and I had this urgent need to spend more time with him. I wasn't ready to say goodbye, and maybe he wasn't either. He insisted on leaving when I did. We said our goodbyes to the bride and groom and to the last guests still lingering. Sofía didn't say a word, but the way she looked at us made it clear she sensed something was about to happen.

Side by side, we walked the cobblestone path that led from the wedding garden to the hotel reception. It was narrow, lined with trees and shrubs, lit only by a few small lanterns. The soft murmur of the wedding and distant music still echoed in the background. Yazid walked next to me without touching me, but once we turned the corner and were out of sight, he wrapped his arm around me and pulled me close."Lola, I want to spend the night with you. Will you come to my hotel? I'm staying in La Jolla," he said, taking a breath. "I feel like we've already lost too much time over the years, and I don't want to let tonight slip away too."

"I don't know what to say…" I smiled shyly, teasing him a little.

"You're terrible at pretending," he said with a nervous laugh. "You're dying to be with me and kiss me. I could tell the moment I saw you."

"You haven't lost an ounce of that self-confidence, have you?"

"So, are you coming?"

"If you insist…" I replied, stepping a little closer to him.

It was hard to hide how much I wanted the night to continue with him. I was glad he felt the same. We'd both been pretending for far too long.

Twenty-four hours earlier, I would've thought this was impossible: first, running into Yazid at Sofía's wedding, and then ending up at his hotel. It felt like one of my best dreams, a déjà vu from the past.

We kept our composure in the cab, for as long as we could. At one point, Yazid started running his hand along my leg under my dress, moving dangerously high up my thigh. I shivered at his touch but stopped him, embarrassed by the idea of the driver noticing.

The ride felt endless, but we finally arrived at his hotel. It was right on the beachfront, just a few blocks from mine. We took the elevator in silence, facing each other, devouring one another with our eyes. Yazid moved closer and closer, I was struggling to hold back. I knew that the second our lips touched, I'd lose my sense of reason and all track of time. Before it went too far, I pointed toward the security camera with a smile. Yazid laughed and looked straight at me.

"You know we're being watched," I said with a nervous giggle.

"Thank God you said that, because all I can think about is taking that dress off you," he said, running his fingers across my lips. "You look amazing. Honestly, the more I look at you, the more beautiful you seem."

"Yazid…"

We walked down the hallway, lined with red carpet and soft lighting, to his room. He closed the door, took off his shoes and blazer, and pulled me close, wrapping me in his arms as he kissed my neck.

"Lola… I missed your scent. I missed you," he whispered. His hands moved slowly down my back until they found the zipper of my dress. "I've dreamed of this moment every night since that cold January morning in 2017."

"And I've missed you too… I still can't believe I'm here with you. I thought I'd never see you again," I whispered, unbuttoning his shirt and biting his lip.

That night was an oasis in the drought of our love. We went back to that place where time slipped away while we loved each other, forgetting everything that had once gone wrong. The longing between us was stronger than anything else.

Our bodies no longer listened to reason. It was something neither of us could control, a force greater than us, pure magnetism. We lost ourselves in each other, blurring the boundaries between his skin and mine. As if time hadn't erased a thing, our emotions rose again from the ashes.

Lying in his arms, I realized that the love I felt for him would stay with me forever. It didn't matter how much time passed or how long we went without seeing or speaking to each other; Yazid would always be my Yazid. My habibi. What I felt for him might have been love, but to me, it was more of a sentence than a blessing. I could taste that love, but unless I gave up who I was, I could never have it. That hurt more than if I'd never known it at all.

Naked and wrapped in each other beneath the sheets, we woke up the next morning. It seemed Yazid had already been awake for a while and was deep in thought. As soon as he saw me stir, he didn't hesitate to share what was on his mind.

"Lola, I've missed you so much… Finding you yesterday felt like a gift. I want you to know that nothing's changed about the way I feel for you," he whispered in my ear, gently stroking my back.

"I've missed you too." I leaned in to kiss his neck. "I thought I'd forgotten you, but now that I'm here with you, I realize all I've done is get used to being without you."

"Love," he said, pulling me into his arms, "why did we make things so complicated? Maybe we could try again... start fresh."

I stayed silent, eyes fixed on the ceiling. For a moment, it was tempting. I imagined what it would be like to wake up next to his smile every morning for the rest of my life. I let myself sink into the fantasy, getting used to his hands, his days, becoming his whole world. But then I remembered the truth: reality was different, and the problems that once tore us apart were still there. It was hard to admit, but our worlds were simply too different.

I knew that once the intoxication of love and passion faded into routine, those irreconcilable differences would rise to the surface again. Sooner or later, one of us would have to sacrifice our convictions to keep the peace, and that wouldn't be fair. Yazid needed a simple, devout woman who shared his values. Ideally, someone submissive. Someone who wouldn't mind sharing him with other women and who wanted to devote her life to bearing and raising his children.

I, on the other hand, needed someone who would support my dreams. I needed someone who understood that while family mattered deeply to me, so did my career. I needed a partner who would allow me to grow and evolve, both personally and professionally.

And Yazid wasn't that person.

It was hard to turn him down, but it was the right thing to do. Letting go of the man who, at that moment, felt like the love of my life wasn't easy. But I chose to stay true to my values rather than surrender to his love. Our story would end in San Diego.

We would always carry each other in our hearts and think of one another under the full moon.

Before returning to my hotel, I needed time to reflect on what had just happened, so I went for a walk along the beach. I was still wearing the red dress from the night before, my makeup smudged, but I didn't care. I sat on a bench along the boardwalk and let my eyes drift toward the horizon.

Two planes crossed paths in the sky above, flying in opposite directions. For a moment, it looked like they might collide, but they didn't. Each one continued on its way. From where I sat, they looked impossibly close, but in reality, there were probably hundreds of meters or even kilometers between them.

And that's when I thought of us. And suddenly, everything became clear. Our story had been nothing more than an optical illusion. The distance between Yazid and me had always been there, we just never saw it. In the end, our paths were never meant to meet.

To everyone who's walked this journey of
life by my side,

THANK YOU.

www.ingramcontent.com/pod-product-compliance
Lightning Source LLC
Chambersburg PA
CBHW070900250626
47159CB00003B/1131